DEVIANT

USA Today Bestselling Author
DANI RENÉ

Black Mountain Academy. From the outside, it may look perfect and ideal—school uniforms, exemplary teachers, privileged students.

But anyone on the inside could tell you about the debauchery, the scandals, the drama, the forbidden–taboo–romances.

Because where Black Mountain Academy is concerned… never judge a book by its cover.

For more information, visit our collection's website
black-mountain-academy.com

PLAYLIST

Would Anyone Care - Citizen Soldier
Impatient - Dark Signal
My Type - Saweetie
When We Make Love - Trey Songz
Na Na - Trey Songz
Twisted Games - Night Panda
Bad Decisions - Trey Songz
King - Niykee Heaton
lovely - Billie Eilish, Khalid
bad guy - Billie Eilish
everything i wanted - Billie Eilish
Fuck it I love you - Lana Del Rey
Guest Room - Echos
Mask - Niykee Heaton

For the full playlist head to Spotify

DEDICATION

*To the good girls who love to be bad and aren't ashamed
to admit it. This one is for you!*

Mad love,
Dani xo

PROLOGUE

ARABELLA

Two months ago

One heartbreak.

One choice.

One mistake.

And my life has taken a turn, and I'm no longer the girl my dad raised. Haven't been for a long time, and now I'm the reason he's no longer here. My father was everything to me, my rock and foundation. And now he's gone. The police officer paces in front of me, back and forth, left and right. I can't swallow. My heart is thudding painfully in my throat, threatening to choke me.

They all know who I am. In this city, Dad's name is everything, and my face on camera is proof that I'm in big shit. I know they'll be wanting a payout to let me go, but with the news they just delivered, I'm not sure they'll get what they want.

I fucked up.

I broke my promise.

What the hell did they expect me to do?

Act normal when they told me I'm being shipped off to some shithole town?

My folks pulled me into the living room two days ago, telling me that they're sending me to some academy. It's bullshit, and they know it. They didn't want me around when my dad's about to run for office. I have a feeling my mother is behind it, more so than dad. She doesn't want me around, and it's not a secret.

I was furious.

I refused to go.

But the law had been laid down.

Instead of being the dutiful daughter and agreeing to go to Black Mountain Academy where my mom and aunt attended school, I fought back and partied for two days straight. That was until a couple of hours ago when I was arrested for something I never should have done.

Anger surges through my veins, but the more I attempt to focus on what they're telling me, I can't because all I can think about is the shit I'm in. I could go to jail. I could be sent away to somewhere far worse than an elite school in the middle of the mountains. I have two months before I'm nineteen. Having to repeat my senior year will be embarrassing enough, but now I may not even be able to do that.

I don't want to be sent to prison.

"And she's going to take primary custody of you while you're in Black Mountain." The words break through my panic, and I snap my gaze up at the large, burly man with a receding hairline and salt-and-pepper moustache that makes me shudder.

"What?" I ask instead.

His dark eyes glare at me with annoyance, which glints with the frustration of someone interrupted mid-coitus. The thought would usually make me want to laugh, but I don't.

3

Instead, I bite the inside of my cheek to remind myself what a shitshow I've gotten myself into. This is real fucking life, not some kid's game gone wrong. I'm eighteen, and they could try me as an adult.

"Your aunt, she's your mother's sister. Your mother has given us her contact details, and we managed to track her down when she was home in Black Mountain. I spoke to her earlier, and she's agreed to the terms. You'll be able to stay with her and finish your senior year."

My brows furrow in confusion. "What about my mother?"

The officer shakes his head, his face a picture of pity and sadness as his moustache twitches. Frustration at my mother burns through my veins. Emotion trickles down my spine, settling inside me, seeping into my bones, and I know what he's going to say before he even says it.

He doesn't look at me; he's no longer glaring directly at me when he finally responds, "She's agreed to have you live with your aunt until you graduate."

"I'll be nineteen in a few weeks. Can't I live on my own? I have my trust fund, which I can live off while I finish school," I inform him. I'm sure I could live on my own. I mean, it can't be too hard. My inheritance will ensure I'm taken care of until I can find a job.

"You'll stay with Midge Olivier until you finish your school year, or you're welcome to finish your senior year while in jail." He turns around as if he's dismissing me to face the other, younger man, who's been observing our conversation from the corner in his uniform.

"That … I can't … That makes no sense. Can I speak to my mother?" Fear laces my words. Usually, I'm a pain in the ass, I admit that, but fear is slowly sinking into my chest, causing my stomach to twist into knots.

Mr. Moustache glances over his shoulder, annoyance etched into his expression as if I were a wayward child. He spins on his heel before his fist slams on the table. Looming over my much smaller frame, the anger on his face says it—I'm lucky to even get this option.

"Your name, your public persona, has been splashed all over the front pages of every newspaper in the city. Spoilt brats should be put in a jail cell," he sneers. I can't deny he's right.

I am spoiled. I am a brat. But I don't respond to him; instead, I lower my head in guilt and try to keep the burning tears at bay.

The agony lodged in my throat chokes me, just like the salty emotion that stings my eyes. I've been taught to keep my pain in check, instead plastering a cool, aloof expression in place.

"I thought so," he utters before he pushes to full height, and I can't stop the shiver from taking hold of my body.

At first, I thought he seemed cool, as if he were trying to be nice, but right now, anger overrides all my thoughts, and I notice how he looks at me, as if I'm lucky. And I am. There's no doubt about it.

My lashes are heavy, and if I blink, the tears will fall. In my mind's eye, I see my dad. The man who was always there for me, no matter what. And I know he'll no longer be there to bail me out of shit. My mother is the ice queen. The heartless, emotionless bitch. But Dad, he was my hero, the one who would love me unconditionally. He's gone. The realization slams into me like a freight train, and my breath is stolen for a long moment.

All the love, the security, everything is gone. The fact that he's no longer here to bail me out of trouble has my stomach flipping over, a reminder that I'm actually alone. I can't depend on my mother. She's never wanted me.

I was Daddy's princess.

But with this shitshow I've gotten myself into, I've disappointed him. He can't see it. I know he would only shake his head with sadness. My lips tremble, and even though I fight the tears, one lone salty path of pain trickles down my cheek when I realize just how broken I truly am.

"Listen to me, Ms. Davenport. Being angry is fine, so is being sad, or heartbroken," Detective Moustache tells me when I don't respond. "But making a mess of your life is not the way to do it. So, what would you like to do?"

I can't *not* go to Black Mountain. I'm the mistake my mother doesn't even want to raise. Before my thirteenth birthday, it was different. She did love me, but it was such a long time ago, at least it feels as if it was. But slowly, I think she came to realize my father loved me more than he did her.

"Ms. Davenport?" The detective cautions again, and I lift my watery gaze to his cool, aloof one. At this point, my only option is to go with my aunt. And if that doesn't work out, once I'm nineteen, I can book a plane ticket and run as far as possible.

"I'll go to Black Mountain," I whisper as the festering guilt and unbearable defeat crush my soul. And it's clear in my tone as the words tumble from my lips.

He nods, looking pleased with himself for ensuring I made the right choice. But is it? I can't know that until I'm there. Perhaps a fresh start where nobody knows me is what I need. Being in a brand-new town sounds like the answer, but that's only if everyone doesn't find out my secret. If they do, I'll be fucked once more.

It's all bullshit.

But I'll do it.

HER

THE PAST

I didn't realize just how ominous this day was until I stepped off the plane moments ago. Now that I'm in the back seat of the car, I see everything and nothing. The storm clouds overhead remind me that this wasn't my choice as much as I was forced into it.

I wanted to run.

I wanted to hide.

But I knew this is where I'm meant to be. Not because of the second chance I'm receiving, but because he *is here, and I'm going to make him see me. For the first time in a long while, I feel as if my life is going to work out.*

But things don't always go according to plan.

Darkness descends as the car winds its way into the town. It's eerie out. The moon is hidden by the clouds that hang heavily, threatening rain on the way. And I wish I could stand in the upcoming downpour and bask in the wetness hoping it will wash my sins away.

But I know it won't.

Nothing can take away the bad things I've done.

As I'm taken home, my lungs struggle to take in air. We weave closer, and I inhale a deep breath, trying to calm my erratic heartbeat. The moment the car pulls to a stop and the familiar three-story home comes into view, I smile. Even in the dimly lit night, I can see the foreboding building waiting for me. There are secrets within the walls of the house that will never be released.

Three floors of rooms filled with opulence.

My new life.

Vastly different from where I'm coming from.

And I know nothing can stop the deviance that simmers through my veins.

ELIAN

Present Day

It only takes a moment for your life to change.

A split second for everything to be turned on its head.

I had to learn how to shut off the misguided notions of normalcy when I chose a new life over the one I grew up in. Grief is a shadow that follows me, and to this day, it still lingers. I don't have space for anything else—not happiness, not love. Emotions, feelings, whatever you want to call them have no home for an enigma like me.

I tried it once and internally grimace at the

memory.

In college, I thought I could be *normal*, and the girl who did manage to find a man underneath the cold, hard exterior did the one thing I can never forgive—she broke her loyalty to me. But if I'm truthful, it wasn't all her fault. I'm not the easiest person to be with. But I did and do expect loyalty above all.

My mind is not my own most times, and when the darkness consumes me, I must allow it to seek its pleasure in ways that would make most women balk. I don't frequent clubs where my needs can be met, so I focus on my career.

I've learned women aren't who they say they are with their fake pristine smiles and shiny veneers. It's nothing but a front, an act, a part they play so well. Moving to Black Mountain, I found them in spades. The bored housewives who fucked the pool boy for breakfast and the gardener for lunch.

Loyalty is everything. And if I can't find that in your pretty gaze when you bat those extra-long lashes at me, it isn't happening. If you can't control yourself once, what's to say it won't happen again? And that's the reason I'm alone in Black Mountain.

Once I finished my degrees in History and English, I found myself wanting to teach. I never thought I would feel comfortable standing in front of students who looked up to me because I'm far from perfect.

I break everything I touch.

My past is littered with the scraps of pain and heartache I can no longer piece together. Human need allows us to make choices based on our desires, and in doing so, we're torn apart, broken, and left for dead.

I have allowed myself to fall prey to those desires one too many times. It doesn't take much for the guilt to gnaw at my insides, for it to feast on my pain, my agony. And as I step foot inside my classroom, I know that *my* choices brought me here.

After leaving Miami, I completed my studies at Stanford University, but even being away from my home, destruction followed. My father's death was hard. It broke me because I never got to say goodbye to him. I never had the chance to tell him all the things he needed to hear from his eldest son.

Christmas Eve will always haunt me. I stepped into the house overlooking the ocean, and that's when the call came. Ahren, my foster brother, had left for college, and even though he wasn't blood, I knew it would gut him as much as it did me. All our lives, Ezra Donati was a father who raised us with an iron fist, but he also loved us unconditionally.

He was taken from us, killed, murdered in cold blood.

Shot by a *colleague* in broad daylight, left for dead while meeting with a man he trusted. And the guilt that will always weigh on me is that I never got to tell him that I'm sorry for not wanting to be a part of his organization. I never felt the need to become what he was.

As soon as the house in Miami was sold, I never looked back. I took myself to the middle of nowhere, a town where I could hide but also live. When I arrived in Black Mountain a couple of years ago, I knew I could never go back. But the town now allows me the opportunity to exact my revenge. It will allow me to find the man who killed my father.

Even though Ahren lives close by, I haven't

told him the real reason I've come here. Being on my own has its privileges. I've enjoyed it, more than I care to admit. I'm able to work, doing something I love, and I'm able to enjoy the solace the town has offered.

The residents of Black Mountain enjoy their privacy. They pay enough for the homes and school fees. So, instead of living in a bustling city, I now find myself in a small, quiet town where my plan will come together soon enough.

And on top of that, I'm allowed the one thing I need to play out my revenge—seclusion. Soon, the rage that's plagued me will come to an end, and I'll be able to find the person I've been seeking for years.

"Ah, Mr. Donati. I just wanted to let you know you have a new student joining today. She's just moved to Black Mountain and will be finishing her senior year with us," states the man who enters the room, interrupting my thoughts. I've heard the whispers from the girls in class about the principal. We're about the same height, coming face to face, and I wonder just how he came to Black Mountain.

Dawson has been good to me. He offered

me a chance at starting over. I haven't told him why I wanted this job or why I came to Black Mountain. Nobody needs to know that.

"Mr. Dawson," I greet, offering him my hand, which he accepts and we shake. *Strong, confident, and commanding.* That's what my father used to tell me. It's what he would say when he taught me how to *be a man,* but even in his teachings, he failed to educate me on just how life can go horribly wrong when you least expect it. "Good to hear that. I'm always happy to help new students who are interested in history. Do you have her file?"

"Yes," Dawson acknowledges as he hands over the folder, which I set on the desk to go through later. "Just keep in mind, she's living with an aunt here in town," he whispers, lowering his tone even though there are no other people around us. I have a free period before the last class of the day comes in, which has allowed me some quiet time. "We want to ensure she's comfortable and no mention of her father who has passed on."

"That's not a problem at all. I know how it feels to be in that situation, so I'll be thoughtful when addressing her. Do you know what happened?" I ask, my brows furrowing in worry.

"Her mother informed us that it was a home invasion. Quite scary if you ask me. That's why I can never live in a city. Prefer the smaller town myself," Dawson confesses with a deep, resounding tone. "If you need anything," he cautions, lowering his tone further as the bell rings. "Like I said, my door is always open."

He shakes my hand once more before he disappears, and I'm left to ponder his words. The girl must be broken inside. Losing a parent isn't easy, especially when you're meant to be finishing your final year in school. Focus is imperative.

I may only be thirty, which is probably considered old by most of my students, but I love what I do. I'll ensure she studies hard and she passes her exams. A strict regimen will hopefully set her on the right path. And until I meet her, I can't tell if she'll be a handful or not.

Hopefully, the latter.

I'm a teacher first, and I'm not here to make friends, but I hope our mutual heartache will allow her to trust me. Last year was difficult.

The students here are mostly wealthy brats who grew up with a silver spoon in their mouths. Since she hasn't been a resident of Black Mountain for long, perhaps she'll be different.

At least, I hope she will.

I pull out my cell phone, tapping out a message to a *friend* I've been seeing. We were meant to meet up tonight, but right now, the only thing I can think about is going home and spending the night alone to read through the details from my private investigator.

Dating isn't something I do. Women are there for a reason—to enjoy for an evening, and when the morning comes, they can leave without me worrying about getting myself into a relationship. Loneliness is something I've become accustomed to. Most times, it doesn't bother me, but there are nights I feel it. Right down to my bones.

Shaking my head to clear it of the worry, I grab the stack of papers and move around the class as I set them down on the desks. Today, we'll be focusing on our first lesson of the year, where I'm able to get into the students' minds.

I'm sure they'll be unhappy with getting

a paper to write on their first day, but it will hopefully allow me to get into their minds and find out what makes them tick. Thankfully, Dawson has given me free reign on my subject, and I can teach in my own way.

I promised myself I will keep myself busy while at work and only focus on finding my father's murderer in my private time. And today is the day my plan slowly comes into play. I've come to Black Mountain for a reason. And I'll make sure it's not a wasted opportunity.

Back at the front of the class, I take out the textbook and place it on my desk along with a notebook and a couple of pens. The register with the names of the students lies waiting for me, but I don't pick it up. Not yet. I want to learn about them before I see their names. Something about judging people just by the family name doesn't sit well with me. Even though it's how I was raised, I never want to do it to my class.

My father always made sure he knew who my friends were. Last names meant more to us than anything else. And loyalty was a currency we had to barter with, even if we hated each other. The rules we learned as children were so strict it felt as if we were imprisoned, but it was all our father could do to keep us safe.

At college, things changed. I had moved away from being a Donati in Miami and instead became a student nobody knew. And Black Mountain has become a town I can find myself in. Where I can learn who I really am.

The door creaks open as the loud, chattering students file into class, some still staring at phone screens, others focused on their friends, yet others rushing through the entrance to grab a desk of choice. Chastising myself for not having time to look at the folder, I shove it into my drawer for later.

I move to the exit once everyone has seated themselves. I'm about to shut the door when a student crashes into me, slamming right into my chest. When I look down, I note how small she is. Delicate. Possibly five-five, which puts her chest height with me. Her hair is a golden blonde, like honey, hanging in waves down her back. Her head tips upward. Eyes the color of granite peek up at me from under long lashes.

There's a hint of makeup on her eyelids when she blinks, a soft blue. The winged liner that frames those orbs of gray makes her expression seem cat-like. But it's her plump lips that capture my attention. They shimmer with pinpricks of glitter when she smiles shyly.

"I-I'm s-sorry, I-I couldn't find the class." Her soft voice lures me into a net, and I step back as if she's electrocuted me. *What the fuck?* "Mr. Donati? This is history, right?"

Finding my voice, I grit out, "Yes, take a seat." Familiarity hits me right in the chest because I have a feeling the folder in my drawer is all about her. I didn't think she'd be in my class. Of all the fucking rooms in this school, she's in mine.

She lowers her head before scurrying into the room. The scent of her perfume lingers. A hint of strawberries catches my nose. I could inhale her fragrance all day and night. The realization catches me off guard, and I slam the door shut. The resounding thud brings instant silence in the room, and all eyes are on me.

It's what my father always wanted from us. I was taught from a young age that children must not be heard. Turning to face the class, I give them a moment to settle, books out, eyes locked on me at the front of the room.

"I hope you're all well versed in writing papers, because I have something for you today," I tell them. "In this classroom, we will be talking about topics you may not be interested in, but you will be graded on your time spent in this room, on your papers you hand in, and the exams you write." I turn, picking up a piece of chalk and do what I've seen teachers and professors do when they're introducing themselves—I write my name in large, scrawled script on the blackboard.

Glancing at the class, I immediately seek her out. The walking disaster I'm drawn to. She's tempting, taunting me with her innocent expression. Undeniable energy crackles through me, through the room. It's as if she were the sun and I were Icarus, and at any moment, I would burst into flames from her heat.

"For your first assignment," I start, allowing a grin to grace my expression as the groans of annoyance rumble through the classroom. "I want you each to tell me why you think history is so important to the modern world. A short paper, two thousand words. And I want it done by tomorrow when you walk through that door." I point at the entrance before pinning *her* with a steely glare. "On time."

A blush turns her cheeks bright pink, her lips purse into a pout, and her eyes shimmer. For a moment, I wonder if she's going to cry, and the sadistic part of me wants nothing more than to see her sadness. I hunger to see her pain, but she squares her shoulders, holding her head high, refusing to cower under my glare as she regards me with indifference.

I smirk at her bravery. The fire in her stare makes every nerve in my body ignite with the need to break her. Just like I planned. If she only knew who she was challenging.

Focusing on the class, I state, "Now that you all know what your homework is, let's begin." Clapping my hands together, I flip open the textbook I studied over the past few weeks. Time to focus and stop myself from staring at the little disaster that is my new student.

ARABELLA

His blue eyes pierce me like daggers straight to the chest. Time ticks by slowly as Mr. Donati teaches his lesson. His deep, gravelly tone sends warm shivers down my spine. He commands the room, and I watch his plump and perfect lips enunciate each word. I have a feeling one of my favorite subjects, history, will now be my most torturous. Not because I don't think I can pass his class, but because the man is distracting.

I've only ever had one boyfriend, and he was a boy. Mr. Donati is a man. One far too old and out of my reach for me to even consider. But that doesn't stop my mind from daydreaming about how his lips would feel against mine.

If I were back home, I wouldn't think twice

about teasing him to the point of no return. But I promised my aunt I'd be good, I'd behave, because she's giving me a second chance. I'm not in jail or some shit, and that's something I am thankful for.

By the time I'd turned sixteen, I was partying with friends, drinking, and even smoking the odd joint. I'm far from a *good girl,* and that's why my parents wanted to send me away. My mother agreed to this move because she knew I was on a path of self-destruction.

"Hi," a whisper comes from beside me. "I'm Marleigh," the girl with long, brown hair says while holding out her hand, and I'm thankful for the distraction from staring at our teacher.

"I'm Arabella," I tell her. "New here."

"I know." She nods, a smile lighting up her face. "I figured. I haven't seen you around before. Welcome to Black Mountain, the Academy with more hot guys than a reality TV show."

I can't help but laugh at that. "Well, then it seems I'm in the right place."

"Definitely. Listen, if you need anything, like a BFF or something similar, my applications are currently wide open." Her laugh is soft, but it's infectious as she grins at me playfully.

"Let me know where to sign up." I offer her a smile. She's the first person I've met so far who's not been stuck up their own ass, and I hope that all the girls are like this. In my last school, the female population didn't like me. I find it easier being one of the guys than on the cheer squad. But with a fresh start, I hope I'm able to find my own tribe of women.

A crash against the wooden surface of Mr. Donati's desk has me jumping in my seat before his voice follows. "Listen up, students, when you're in my class," Mr. Donati says with his seething gaze locked on me, slamming me right to the back of the chair. "I want your focus on me. On the blackboard. Not on your phone. Not on your friends. Am I understood?" He poses the question to the class, but he doesn't look away.

"Yes, sir," I find myself responding as if he were shouting. I don't even have my phone. Auntie Midge said to leave it at home so I can focus on my first day. Thankfully, I listened to her.

"Now, when you think about history, I know

most of you consider it old bullshit you don't want to know about," he informs us, earning a few gasps and sniggers from the students. I'm shocked as well. I've never had a teacher who was so open about cursing in his class. "For those who are new to my class, I run a tight ship, and I expect you to put the work in, but I do want you to learn when you're in this room."

One of the girls a few desks over raises her hand. And for a moment, I think he's going to ignore her, but instead, he nods toward her.

"I'd like to know if you're single, Mr. Donati," she muses, a grin plastered on her face. Her long, blonde hair is pinned in a ponytail, and her perfectly manicured hands are folded on the desk as if she didn't just flirt with our teacher.

"My personal life has nothing to do with any of you," Donati bites out. He doesn't seem perturbed by her question, and I wonder briefly if he's had students coming on to him before.

"It's a shame. I may need a date for the prom," blondie tells him, teasing a pen over her plump, glossy lips. The rest of the class laughs, but I don't. My fingers tighten around my pen, and my stomach drops at the thought of him with her. She's the type of girl he'd go for if he were so inclined. She's gorgeous with a perfect figure, and she looks like she could be a runway model.

Whereas I try to play coy, unless there's someone I want to impress. Or catch the attention of. I've spent my life being the center of attention, especially when it comes to guys. Most girls back home would call me a slut, and they did, for a long while. Where I'm from, shaming women for being into sex is one insult the girls loved to throw around if you weren't shy to dress up.

But right now, I'm thankful that we have to wear this god-awful uniform because I *dressed* it up—black skirt, the white shirt which fits a little too tight shows off the black bra I'm wearing underneath. The unwelcome noose of a tie which chokes me, along with the blazer sporting the school crest on the breast pocket. At least nobody truly stands out too much, and nobody can assume you're trying to get attention, unless you're me where I've intentionally shortened the skirt from the frumpy length to mid-thigh.

"When you're in my class, you will respect me. You will also focus on your schoolwork. So, Miss …?" he says, looking directly at blondie as he waits for her to tell him her name.

"Oh, it's Melody Vanderbilt," she tells him. "But you can call me Melody, sir." Her tone lowers into a seductive purr at the word *sir*. But with a glance at Mr. Donati, he doesn't seem at all affected.

"Miss Vanderbilt, I trust you'll behave in my class. If not, you're welcome to visit the principal's office." The cold tone of his voice sends a shiver down my spine, causing me to tremble. "And that goes for anyone else in my class. Here, we learn to be professional, to ensure that when we step out of this class into the big, shitty world beyond, we know how to conduct ourselves."

His gaze once again roves over the class, and I hold my breath. I can't explain it, but I want his eyes on me. I'm sorely disappointed when he doesn't even look my way. It's stupid. I feel like a child, crushing on a man way out of my league.

But that's never stopped me before.

And I have a feeling Mr. Donati will become my new favorite teacher.

The sinking sun is still warm as I make my way home from my first day of school. Walking up the street from Black Mountain Academy in my short skirt and knee-high leggings causes attention to skitter my way. Ignoring the stares, the whispers, and the snickers from the other students, I make my way up the road.

I haven't been the *new girl* before, and it's uncomfortable. Everyone seems to speak in hushed tones when I walk past as I head up the hill toward the road which will take me to my aunt's multi-million-dollar mansion.

I grew up around wealth and false promises that were made to show off how *perfect* my family was. Nothing lasts forever—either it's taken from you, or you die. Either way, I'm no longer holding onto hope, and I'm certainly not believing of people who offer promises and bullshit wrapped up in a neat little bow.

Overnight, my life was flipped on its head when the cop cars pulled up to the house and they raided the party. I shouldn't have been there, but I was. Caught on camera by a paparazzi asshole with my panties in hand, sandwiched between two of my best guy friends. It looked worse than it was.

I stop for a moment to take in the academy from my viewpoint. It's an impressive building for a high school. But, considering the annual fees to attend classes here, I'm not surprised. I watch students mill around the parking lot, all in cliques. They've clearly been friends their whole lives, and there I was, a girl new to the world they've grown up in.

Being used to the city life is leaving me slightly jarred by the small town where everyone seems to know each other. Even though I grew up in the public eye, living in a city allowed me to disappear when I wanted it.

Solace is a luxury that's hard to come by. Most people pay a lot of money for it. It seems Black Mountain has decided to offer it to me on a silver platter.

"Ara!" My name is screeched from behind me, causing me to spin on my heel. Marleigh, the girl from class, comes racing toward me.

When we met in history, she seemed nice enough. I wasn't expecting her to make good on her promise of being friends, but as she grins, racing toward me, I wonder if perhaps I was too quick to judge.

Her sleek, brown hair shimmers in the slowly dying sunlight. "I wanted to see if you'd be up for a party this weekend." She's panting breathlessly as she reaches me. "I spoke to a few friends, and it's going to be epic."

"I don't know. Parties are not really my thing," I lie, already feeling the anxious nerves twisting in my stomach. The last time I went out and got drunk, I ended up cuffed in a police station. I still can't believe my actions got me caught, but then again, breaking into someone's home to party it up as revenge isn't the best thing I could've done. Only, nobody knew we'd picked the locks, that was our secret. Knowing that my name and face was most certainly recognizable in the city, I still went ahead, got drunk, and got caught.

"Oh, come on," she coaxes. "You're new here, and you need to meet people. It's at this epic mansion on the outskirts of town. A hot tub, swimming pool, even a freaking home cinema." She sounds so excited, and I wouldn't want to let her down.

I don't have to go overboard. And I doubt the kids here would be anything like the ones back home. However, I'm not sure Aunt Midge would be all too happy to have me racing out to party my first weekend in town.

I shrug slowly. "I can chat with my aunt. I'm living with her while I'm here." Not a complete lie, more of an omission. I guess a party wouldn't hurt. But I do need more information because I know Aunt Midge will be giving me the third degree the moment I mention it. "Whose house is it?"

"One of the guys who used to attend the academy, Alistor Barrington. He's in college now, which means hot older guys," she tells me with a cheeky wink. "Also, he has a best friend I'm almost sure will be perfect for you." Her grin is dazzling as she bounces on her tiptoes with excitement shining in her eyes. I know I can't refuse because it's all sounding too good. "I think we both need to have some fun, and everyone will want to meet you. These parties are always the talk of the school for a week after. So, what do you say? Want to join me for a bit of destructive behavior for one night?"

"Let me see what the deal is back home with my aunt. I'm not promising anything. She's strict." Another lie. "But I will try my best to get her to allow me freedom for one night." I can't tell Marleigh just why I may *not* be able to come out, but for now, my excuse will have to do.

"You have to come, so even if she says no, I'll visit and tell her how imperative it is for you to be there. I mean, it's senior year and parties are what the next few months are made for." She seems convinced, and to be honest, since my dad died three months ago, I haven't been able to have fun. The closed casket funeral never allowed me to say goodbye. It may seem strange, but I needed to see his face, but my mother was adamant that I couldn't. So, instead of saying goodbye, I was left with the emptiness of never being able to see him one last time.

Each time I think about that day, I fall to pieces. Perhaps this will be a good thing.

"Sounds good," I tell Marleigh, who's grinning like a fool.

"That's my girl," she responds, hooking her arm in mine and walking up the road with me as we head farther away from school.

But with every step, I can't stop recalling his tall, broad frame. The way his shirt seemed to tease at the strong arms underneath. His muscled legs in dark slacks and his ass that looked like you could bounce a penny off it as he moved through the class.

The memory of his perfectly manicured hands with hints of veins peeking from the tanned skin. Strong, foreboding, but ultimately sexy. But it was also his stare as he watched me whenever he didn't think I noticed. It pierced me right through my chest.

I have a crush.

Mr. Donati is forbidden.

I shouldn't *want* him.

But my mind has a life of its own.

HIM

THE PRESENT

He's smiling. She looks beautiful as she sits opposite him. I hate that his eyes are on her. I don't like it one fucking bit. But then again, if she were looking at me like that, I'm not sure I could handle it.

My mind spins with all the possibilities. I smile when I see the shiver that trickles down her body. I want nothing more than to give her that myself. To feel her silken skin as I mar her creamy flesh.

The darkness has always swirled through me. I never liked women who did what she does. Open their filthy legs for every other man including the one giving her everything she wants. The time has come for her secrets to be divulged. The shiny veneer will soon be tarnished by the truth.

It all starts with a lie.

It compounds itself. Once you tell one, you must cover up with another and another. And slowly, the more you dig yourself into that grave, the darker it becomes as you bury yourself under a mound of filth.

They rise from their seats, hands entwined, and I smile. She didn't think I'd be here, watching, waiting. I've bided my time for so long that I'm vibrating with the need to finish this. It ends tonight because he'll learn all there is to know about her.

I close my eyes and picture it, the thick yellow folder on the small welcome mat of his estate. Perhaps the maid has already retrieved it and set it on his desk. And maybe he won't see it the moment he walks in. I pray he fucks her before that. I pray that his dick is deep inside her as he spills his seed before he learns the truth.

One last hoorah before he walks away for good.

And then I can step in. Just like I always planned.

ELIAN

I stare at my brother. We're polar opposites. With his motorbike, bad-boy attitude, and tattoos, he looks like he belongs in a motorcycle gang. I guess his dream to become a professional tattoo artist will come to fruition, which I don't doubt. He'll even look the part.

"You're acting like a teenager," I tell Ahren. He's an adult now, and I can't tell him what to do, but the thought of him joining a fucking biker gang doesn't calm me down. Perhaps I should call up some friends over in Thorne Haven. They'll give him something to think about.

But I don't want Ahren near Creed Haven. Perhaps I should rethink this. Even though my foster brother has a good head on his shoulders about finishing school, it's the danger that comes with putting on a kutte and heading into the unknown that leaves me worried.

"I'm young. I want to enjoy my twenties," he tells me confidently, shrugging into the black leather jacket I know hides his ink. When he got into college, he started getting artwork all over his body. His art is his life, and I'm thankful he has something to focus on. Losing my dad was hard on him as well. And I know it's a topic we don't always talk about, but I love him as if he were my blood.

"Parties aren't the be all and end all of college. Studying is. Even though you're acing your art classes, you have to be responsible." I know I sound like a parent, but I can't help it.

He turns away, looking out over the expansive garden. My home is meagre compared to some of the neighbors, yet I have a about three acres here.

"Growing up wasn't easy for me after losing my folks. Thankfully, your dad gave me a life, a second chance, I don't want to fuck that up, Eli," he tells me, confidence brimming in his tone as he sips his coffee. "I hear you have a few hotties in your class this year." He drops the query like I knew he would. I know why he's asking, but I don't focus on it. At least, I try not to.

"I suppose," I respond, keeping my voice cool. "Why?" I ask, even though I already know the answer. He has a few friends in this senior class. Even though he never set foot on the grounds today, the football team is just some of the guys he hangs out with when they're partying at his friend Alistor's house. The asshole is richer than God, and his folks leave him alone at home so much you'd think he was an orphan.

"Alistor and I were meeting a few guys from the team," Ahren informs me with a smirk sweeping across his expression. "One in particular did catch my eye."

"Oh?" I act disinterested, but I'm far from it. My body is rigid because I have a feeling I know which one it is. One thing we've learned over the years is that my brother and I have the same taste in women.

"Sleek, honey-colored hair down to her bubble butt, nice curves, pouty lips. And wearing the school uniform, she looked like every college boy's wet dream and every teacher's filthy fantasy." He sounds far too fucking satisfied with himself because he knows he's on touchy ground with me.

"Don't start that bullshit."

"Why? Are you trying to tell me you didn't notice how her skirt kisses those thighs I know you want to spread?" His challenge is clear. Asshole. Sometimes, we fight and argue, but I love him, deeply. The only person I'll ever offer that feeling to.

"Aren't you late for something?" I bite out as frustration takes hold of me. Ahren chuckles, knowing he has me right where he wants me. Even though I try to school my expression, it doesn't work.

Arabella.

When I saw her name on the roll call, excitement shot through me. But then I noticed it. There's an air of sadness that emanates from her. I must admit, she reeled me in, and I never expected it. She doesn't belong here, in a small town. She should be walking runways. But then again, I never planned on teaching at some rich-kid academy when I could've been traveling the world. But we all make our choices.

"Ahren, she's off limits," I bite out, but I know Ahren notices my shift in demeanor, and from the tone of my voice, it's clear. She's affected me. He can read me like a book, even though everyone else can't see shit going on behind my façade.

"They're eighteen," Ahren tells me easily. His dark eyes land on mine. "You know, teacher-student relationships are frowned upon," he jokes, bumping shoulders with me. Being the older one in our relationship, I've gotten used to his behavior at times, which can be immature. There are moments I wish he'd think about what he says.

"I'm a professional, I don't—"

"Cut the crap, man," he says. "You're into her. I can see it written all over your face. Why don't you come to a party at Alistor's house this weekend? I'll make sure she's there."

"I don't do high school parties," I snap, finally locking my wary gaze on my idiot brother, who looks like he's enjoying taunting me. "And if I'm seen there, I will lose all credibility with the students."

"This isn't your first rollercoaster. Your first few months of teaching, you had one of those pretty girls bouncing on your dick like she was trying to ace her exam."

"It was a mistake. I was stupid enough to break the rules."

He grins. "Rules are meant to be broken, Eli. And most of the students already see you as an equal since you're not ancient like some of the professors we have at college. When I was in my senior year, it was the teachers who gave us the time of day who stuck out to me, that I remember, like you. Not the old, stuck-up assholes who treated us like shit."

"I don't treat them like shit. But it looks like I'm preying on students if I were to party with you." I don't know why I'm so frustrated at Ahren. No. That's a lie. I do know. It's so fucking clear. I'm allowing some little girl to get the better of me. Yes, she's beautiful, but she's too young for me, and I'm her teacher.

"Come to the goddamned party, Eli. There'll be a few college girls as well." It's tempting. A party may not be great when my students are there, but what else is there to do in this town? Most of the single women my age are looking for a ring and a white picket fence. But with Ahren, I don't feel like I'm *that* much older than him, so it won't look strange if I were to attend.

"Fine," I sigh, turning to the garden once more. "Just don't do anything stupid when we're out together. I don't need a reminder than you're my *baby* brother." This time, I taunt him. We only have a seven-year difference, him being twenty-three, but at times, it feels like we're lifetimes apart.

"Baby?" He chuckles before grabbing his crotch. "Hardly. I'm looking forward to it, bro." Ahren grins. "I'll see you on the weekend. And don't be late," he tells me with a mock salute after he sets his empty coffee mug on the table.

I don't want to act like a father and question him about the biker club he's mentioned or the apprenticeship I know he has coming up, so I nod. When I was younger, I would be out at parties till the early hours of the following morning. But this is a new chapter in our lives, and my home is always open to him. Some evenings, Ahren will stay over, but I have a feeling he's got plans tonight.

I glance at the time. It's late, and I need to get ready for work. I make my way indoors and hope I don't have another physical run-in with the beauty today.

Arabella.

Her name elicits thoughts I shouldn't be having. I should be focused on revenge, but there's more to it than that. Perhaps having her here is a gift I should enjoy.

She is bad news. Not only for my libido, but her folder had some interesting things about the little deviant. Even though she looks like a goddamned angel, she's so far from it. And that's the reason I can't stop thinking about her.

Her name has brought up a myriad of emotions in me. Davenport is pure filth, even if she doesn't realize it. I know far too much about her and her family. And even though I wanted nothing more than to watch her cry, to see her pain and bask in it, my desire far outweighs my need to hurt her.

I want the bad girl.

I want nothing more than to corrupt her even further.

My final class of the day piles in, and that's when I finally see her for the first time today. I thought I would luck out, that she'd be off sick, or perhaps have left the goddamned school. But here she is, dressed in her uniform, which has been haunting me since the day she walked in here. The white button-up which doesn't hide the black bra underneath cupping her ample tits. Once again, her skirt swishes against her creamy thighs, and my body responds with a jolt of approval.

"Good afternoon," I greet them and receive a less than stellar response. "Today we're focusing on the Roman War. Let's talk about fighting, soldiers, and bloodshed. Who here has an opinion on why any war would start?"

My gaze tracks each uncomfortable-looking student, ignoring *her*. At least, trying to. But my eyes finally land on Arabella, who's slowly lifting her hand after realizing she's the only one to volunteer. Palm facing me, and I notice her delicate fingers, and I can't stop imagining them wrapped around my cock.

Clearing my throat, I attempt to clear the dirty thoughts from my mind. "Yes, Arabella," I say, tasting her name as if it were a fine wine and I were a connoisseur. I decide for a moment I enjoy the flavor of it but quickly shake the feeling away. This is fucking ridiculous.

"All wars are tragic. They're born of hatred and anger, and of jealousy. Men feel as if revenge is something they should gain, where I feel instead of bloodshed, there are far better ways of dealing with problems," she tells me, passion and confidence emanating from her as she speaks about something she's clearly very interested in. "But then again, their morality had been so twisted by their anger, they don't seem to have cared for what others thought of them."

"So, you're saying just because they killed without remorse and took any woman or man they wanted to bed, they are more interesting?" I challenge, hoping she'll take the bait.

"No. Not at all. I'm saying their lack of consideration at what society would say about them makes them more *human* than God. Who says something is wrong when it *feels* right?

Granted, there are many acts that are illegal and should stay that way, but many times societal taboos are unfounded or even one-sided."

For someone so young, I can't help but be impressed. She's nineteen, but she speaks with such confidence it's impressive. Her eyes are wide, locked on mine.

"In that case, you'll each write a paper on the Roman War and what you would do put in their situation," I tell the class, breaking my stare from the beautiful Arabella and taking each of the other students' expressions in. "Choose one of their stories you find interesting and tell me why you *think* they did what they did. Or better yet, argue how you think it would be seen in our modern-day society."

Groans from around the class make me smile.

"And when you leave today, I'd like your assignments from yesterday," I remind them as I settle behind my desk to continue the rest of the lesson. But each time I do face the class, it's her gaze I capture with mine, and for a split second, I allow myself to think about the possibility of her and me.

And by the time the end of class comes, I'm filled with rage such a beautiful girl could walk in here and tempt me. I've always been in control of every situation I've encountered, but something about her makes all those scales tip in the wrong direction. It shouldn't. It's wrong. And I need to focus on the end game here because getting my dick wet should've been a bonus, not the motivation.

The moment my classroom is empty, I sit in my chair and stare out at nothing. For a long while, I enjoy the silence. Even though there are students milling around outside, laughing and joking, I revel in the silence after a long day, but also in the fact that her perfume seems to have embedded itself in my nostrils.

Ahren is right. I may be her teacher, but I can't deny she's beautiful, perfect even. Her skin looks as smooth as the finest silk, and my fingertips ache to touch her. Her lips are plump, a perfect bow, and her flowing, honey-colored hair that hangs to the middle of her back has me wanting to wrap it around my fists.

And then there are her curves. Those soft, luscious curves I'd love to learn every inch of with my tongue. I know I must restrain my thoughts, but in this moment, I allow myself the freedom to enjoy the desire that's risen inside me.

Tomorrow, I'll be back to normal.

Tonight, I'll find my release to images of her racing through my mind.

ARABELLA

"So, like I told you before, there's Alistor, who owns the house. Well, his folks do, but that's beside the point. They're never there. And Ahren, his best friend who is…" Marleigh is talking, but I haven't been all too focused on her explanation of where we're going tonight. She's focused on the boys, but I can't stop thinking about a certain teacher I shouldn't be thinking of. I wanted to impress him with my love of mythology, and when I handed in my assignment from yesterday, I was sure he noticed me trembling.

I can't explain why, but he makes me nervous. To the point where the hummingbirds in my stomach wake up and fight a battle with my heart. Both thrumming and tumbling with an endless reminder that I most certainly have a crush.

"Are you listening to me?" Marleigh asks, breaking through the fog that has been caused by Mr. Donati and those endless pools I feel myself getting lost in, making it feel as if he's attempting to bore a hole right through me with one single stare.

"No. Yes. I'm just nervous."

"Don't be," Marleigh tells me earnestly. "This is going to be fun, and by fun, I mean we'll be able to just forget about school and focus on dancing the night away." Her enthusiasm is catching, and I have to smile. She's the complete opposite of me. Her wavy, brown hair with those dark eyes are so far from my gray eyes and honey-hued locks.

"I know. I'll be fine once we're actually there and I'm in the throng of people," I inform her with a wink. I slip on the shiny heels that give me a couple inches of height and take in my appearance in the mirror.

My long hair hangs in a sleek style down to the base of my spine. The shimmery black mini dress would most probably give any parent a heart attack, but my aunt isn't home, and thankfully, I'll be able to sneak in before she gets back from her meetings.

At first, I was worried about going back to *that* life. But this is different. At least, that's what I tell myself in the hopes of not allowing guilt to wash over me. Emotions are pointless. That's what I've learned from an early age.

Don't feel them.

Don't show them.

So even as my heart shatters thinking about what I've lost, I haven't cried. I don't allow the tears to fall because it's a sign of weakness. And Dad always taught me weakness is for fools.

"This is so short," I tell Marleigh, looking at the curve of my ass as the hemline hangs at the top of my thighs. "I mean … I can't bend over."

A laugh tumbles from her lips. "Or you could and any guy in his right mind would do anything you ask of him." Her dark brow arches, and the smirk on her lips tells me she's already planned how to get attention tonight.

"You're ridiculous." I can't help but laugh. It's good to have made a connection here. I didn't think I'd have someone I could call a friend on my first day at the academy, but Marleigh has been spending each lunch with me, and the classes we do share, we've sat together, which makes the transition less lonely than I expected it to be.

"And that's why we're going to be the best of friends," she announces as she walks over to me. Her dress is fire-engine red, and it also shimmers under the light as she moves. "Don't worry about a thing, Ara. You will have the most amazing school year. We're seniors. We're meant to cause a little bit of trouble."

And that's what worries me.

By the time we get to the party, it's in full swing. There are students filling every available space. The living room has a table set up where guys are playing beer pong, and we move through the house into the kitchen where we find bottles of alcohol strewn along the countertop. Some labels I recognize, others I don't.

Marleigh grabs two Solo cups, and we fill them with beer from a keg near the sink. The bubbly liquid is bitter tasting, but I sip it down anyway. Marleigh slips her hand in mine, our fingers laced as she pulls me out into the backyard which looks like it could host a music concert it's so big. I'm not sure how many acres of land this is, but it's much more than I'm used to coming from the city.

A hot tub filled with almost-naked bodies is positioned over to the right of the swimming pool, which looks rather inviting with blue lights illuminating it. Girls and guys surround it, sitting on loungers and bean bags while holding drinks in their hands.

There are large vibrating speakers positioned around the outdoor area, giving off the feel of surround sound. The bass rumbles through me; a dance song I don't recognize blares at the guests.

"There he is," Marleigh hisses in my ear, pointing at the bar beside the pool. The guy in question has two full sleeves of ink. His dark hair looks black from here, and he's wearing a pair of black, torn jeans which hang from his tapered hips. Lifting my eyes, I trace them along his toned abs, up to broad shoulders, and find a smile that's bright and welcoming.

"Who's that?" I gesture with my chin toward the guy. His dark hair and eyes with olive skin make him look Mediterranean. Rugged bad boy. That's what he reminds me of. The complete opposite of Mr. Donati.

"Ahren," she says right in my ear. "Come, we'll go and say hello." Before I have time to refuse her, she drags me along, pulling me all the way down to the garden until we reach him. He's standing with a few other guys, but the moment he notices us, he practically ignores his friends and focuses on Marleigh and me.

"Beautiful women at the party. I like it," he says. His voice is a husky tone, which rumbles right through me as deeply as the music does.

"Hi, Ahren," Marleigh greets. Her smile is electric. "How are you?"

"Leigh. I'm good, behaving badly, just like everyone expects me to. Always nice to see you." He tips his head in welcome, then roves his gaze over to me. "And your friend is …?"

"This is Arabella," Marleigh introduces me. "She's new to Black Mountain," she excitedly informs him.

"It's nice to meet you," he says, offering me his hand, which I accept. His grip is firm, commanding. I can't deny he's gorgeous, and the cocky smirk that graces his lips makes my stomach flutter wildly.

"Nice to meet you too. Quite the party you have here."

"Not me. I'm merely a VIP guest. This is all Alistor's doing. He likes to go all out and then some." He waves his hand around, a smile on his lips, and I realize I'm staring when he glances at me once more. Marleigh was right. He could be my type. Perhaps I should give this a chance. "Ah, well, I didn't think you'd be here," Ahren says, his gaze flitting over my shoulder at the person behind us.

The hairs on the back of my neck stand on end. The scent of cologne hits me right in the nose—masculine and spice. It's familiar. I've gotten lost in it each time I've walked into history class. The heat of *him* is right behind me, and as I twist on my heel, I find him glaring down at me.

"Mr. Donati." I voice his name in a whisper that causes me to cringe inwardly. "You're ..." I turn to Ahren, then to Marleigh who's grinning at me like a fool. *She knew he'd be here?* No, she couldn't have. She would've told me. But then again, why would she? I didn't tell her I've been thinking about this man nonstop since I walked right into his solid chest on my first day of school.

"It's Elian," he finally says, breaking through my inward hysterical panic. "We're not at school, and I always try to ensure that I keep my personal and professional life separate." Even though he tells us this, there's still an air of authority wafting from him. I doubt this man knows how to let his hair down.

He's dressed in a pair of dark jeans and a black shirt, which has a few buttons undone at the top, showing off the smooth, tanned skin underneath. With that small glimpse of flesh, I can't stop staring at the way he looks less put together from the way he normally does in class.

"Be careful tonight, girls," he warns us. "And don't overdo those." His stare locks on the Solo cup in my hands, which still has beer in it.

"Oh, come on, Eli," Ahren says from behind

me. "It's a party. Don't be a spoil sport. They can have one or two drinks." I can practically feel the tension between the two men. "Besides, aren't you the cool teach?"

Marleigh grabs my hand and tugs me closer to her. "We're going to dance," she informs them before she drags me behind her until we reach a section of the garden which has been turned into a dance floor. Bodies sway to the music, but even as I join her, trying to get lost in the rhythm that's beating through the speakers, I can't stop my gaze from finding Elian in the crowd.

Even his name is sexy.

"He likes you," Marleigh speaks, once again close to my ear as we dance together. I look directly at her, locking my gaze on hers, and I see no humor reflected there.

Shock must paint my expression when I gasp, "What?"

"He likes you. It's so damn obvious." She shrugs nonchalantly, as if she's just told me the weather report is predicting sunshine all week. My heart catapults at the thought of Elian Donati *liking* me. But he's a man. He's mature, older. There's no way he'd be interested in a senior in high school.

"Who?" The moment I ask, she gives me a don't-fucking-joke-with-me glare.

"Elian Donati," Marleigh announces his name directly to me.

"I think you've had enough to drink," I tease, trying to ignore the fact that my cheeks are burning with embarrassment.

"Something tells me you like him too," she observes with a flirty wink.

"No." I shake my head. "He's a teacher, and that's just weird."

Marleigh tips her head back, laughing out loud at me crinkling my nose for effect. *Can she really see right through my lies?* "I'm sure you weren't just blushing like a tomato because it's weird."

"You're insufferable," I bite out playfully as we sway to the music. Marleigh laughs, but there's a knowing look in her eyes. I can't deny it, and it seems my new friend can see right through my lies.

As the song comes to an end, I excuse myself, telling her I need the restroom, and make my escape. I'm sure Marleigh is about to follow me, but a tall, older guy steals her away, inadvertently distracting her, which I'm grateful for. I need to gather my thoughts.

In the house, I move through the bodies shifting against each other. In the corner of the living room against the soft, comfortable-looking couches are groups of students chattering loudly. I can make out a few words over the chilled, thumping bass of Echoes singing "Guestroom" coming from the surrounding speakers.

The bathroom is locked, and a few shouts come from inside, which makes me laugh. *Occupied.* I make my way toward the entrance hall and find the staircase leading up. The house has a modern touch to it with glass from ceiling to floor and steel railings along the steps, which brings me out onto a landing. I have two options, up or right. I walk along the hallway, moving deeper down the corridor when I spy an empty bathroom.

Locking myself inside, I use the facilities. I'm washing my hands when footsteps sound in the hallway, but whoever is on the other side of the door doesn't knock.

"I told you I can't keep doing this," a voice

says in hushed urgency. "There is an agreement in place, which I would advise you don't break because I don't like people forcing my hand," he states, and I realize I know that voice. I would know it in my sleep. It's Elian Donati. "Black Mountain is off limits to you. I'm not playing kids games with you. What happened is done, it's over, and you need to come to terms with it."

I wait for a response, but all I get is silence. He's obviously talking on the phone, and he doesn't sound happy. I shouldn't be listening in on his conversation, it's private, but I can't help myself. Pressing myself against the door, I lean in and close my eyes in an attempt to focus on his voice.

"That night is over and done. A mistake that I will not repeat. I made a vow to move forward, and I always keep my promises." He sounds angry. The words are practically growled. I wonder if this man ever smiles. "Don't contact me again." The threat hangs in his words, and I can't stop the ice from trickling down my spine.

When it's quiet once more, I take a long, deep breath before opening the door, thinking he's gone, but the moment it whooshes open, I'm met with a glare that scalds me with its heat. My stomach drops to my feet, and I suddenly feel nervous.

"I-I-I'm sorry. I was in here," I mumble, pointing at the bathroom. The rage in his gaze rips me to shreds, and I'm sure if he could touch me, his hands would do the same. His dark brow arches upward, as if he's assessing my words, questioning if I was listening or not. "I'm sorry."

"You seem to apologize a lot," he bites out before taking a step toward me, which has my back hitting the door behind me.

When Elian leans in, his spicy, masculine scent envelops me with warmth, and I can't stop myself from inhaling it deeply. This man affects me more than I'd care to admit, and when his lips brush over my ear, I shiver.

"Perhaps next time you should be careful of eavesdropping on people. It's rude." Before I can find my retort, he's pushing away from me and moving down the hallway, leaving me gaping at his retreating form.

What the fuck just happened?

Any lingering doubts about wanting and

liking Elian Donati that I've been cultivating in my mind are gone in that moment. *He's* rude. He's an overconfident asshole. And if I ever come into contact with him in a personal capacity again, I'll make sure to tell him so.

ELIAN

Bringing the drink to my lips, I sip on the harsh alcohol, enjoying the burn, while my eyes are locked on Arabella. The way her hips sway. How her ass jiggles and those beautiful tits bounce is sinful, distracting. I shouldn't be watching her, yet I can't look away. Ahren knew; he planned this right down to the fucking T. He knows my type because he's seen me with women while we were living in Miami, and Arabella is most certainly it. Everything about her is what I consider perfection. But he doesn't realize who she is and just why she's captured my attention.

"She's quite the temptress. I can't deny she's gorgeous," Ahren says as he joins me on the porch. The tiki torches light up the expanse of the garden. With the blue illumination coming from the swimming pool, it allows the mock dance floor to shine, giving me the perfect view of Arabella.

"I want to know about her. But you're going to do it for me," I tell him as she spins on her heel, her eyes finding mine like a magnet drawn to its polar. I hold her gaze for a moment before tilting my glass in a *cheers* toward her before taking another long swallow. The burn trickles down my throat, warming my stomach, and I know I need to leave soon. The longer I stay, the more I watch her, the more I'm entranced. She isn't going to be easy to walk away from.

"Date night?" Ahren asks, his voice dropping to a whisper, but the excitement in his tone is obvious. He enjoys playing games, just like I do, but this one is different.

"Yeah. Just test the waters. I need to know if she's easily swayed," I tell him. Even though I shouldn't do this, because the last time Ahren and I took a girl, it turned out to be a mistake. But I have a feeling Arabella is different. "I'll see you tomorrow," I tell him. Now that he knows what to do, I can go home. Silence is something I need right now, to figure out how this could even work. I want her, there's no denying it, and when I want something, I always get it.

The only question is—*would she want the darkness I crave?*

"Are you leaving so soon, teach?" Ahren questions when I set the glass down, my focus tugged away from my dancing temptress to my foster brother. The grin on his face is evidence enough just how much he'd like me to linger. And I must be honest with myself. I want to be near her. It's ridiculous, but the more I watch her dancing, the harder I want to fuck her and make her scream my name. I chalk it up to lust. Pure and simple.

She's too young for me. And this will be a fling for her.

Time to break some rules.

"Yeah, you've got this." I don't look at him when I tell him this.

Even though it would be nice to stay, to act as if I'm one of *them*, I'm not. I know Ahren will look out for her, so I'm not worried about leaving. But what does bother me is if she ended up with some college kid who wanted the same thing I do—to get into her panties.

But it's not my place to stop her. I'm not a parent, and I'm certainly not her boyfriend. When Arabella walked out of the bathroom, her eyes wide on mine, I almost lost my shit. The phone call had put me in a foul mood, and this pretty little thing isn't helping one bit.

"Keep an eye on them, and don't do anything stupid," I warn as I walk by him and catch the slow, predatory grin spreading on his face. He nods. I move into the house, making my way to the exit. There are so many people in every corner of the mansion I'm sure when morning comes, it's going to look like a bomb hit the place.

I slide into the driver's seat of my sleek, black Maserati and turn the key in the ignition. I'm pulling out of the parking spot when I see her. She's walking away from the party, alone, and I know I should leave her to it, but deep down, my gut churns.

I come to a stop right in her path, causing her to stumble backward. Her gray gaze locks on mine, and her face twists in shock. I unlock the passenger door and lean over to push it open.

"What are you doing?" she bites out, attempting to look more grown up than her nineteen years. But she's had too many drinks, and I'm not allowing her to walk alone. Even though Black Mountain is safe.

"Taking you home," I snap while waiting for Arabella to set her pert little ass in the seat. I realize I'm angry because she's tipsy. She shouldn't be drinking if she can't handle her liquor. And even though I know *why* she's doing it, I still want to spank her pert ass.

She crosses her arms over her chest, and I can't help my gaze trailing there where I get a glimpse of her cleavage peeking over the neckline of her too-short dress. "I'm not your responsibility."

"Well, you should be someone's fucking responsibility. Now get your ass in the car before I get out and put you in myself." My words leave no room for argument. And for a moment, I expect her to refuse me. She looks pissed enough to tell me to go to hell, but after a long moment, she sighs before slipping into the passenger seat beside me.

"I don't like being treated like a child," she tells me, but she's looking straight ahead.

I lock the doors before speeding out of Alistor's driveway. "If you don't act like a child, you won't be treated like one," I grit out. Frustration has taken a hold of me, and even though I know I'm being a dick to her, I can't help it.

My teeth are clenched so hard my jaw ticks, but I grind down to calm myself. It's not the frustration that she's tipsy; it's the fact that I notice just how short her dress is. The hemline slipping up her smooth, creamy thigh. The scent of her fucking strawberry shampoo, or perfume, or whatever the fuck it is envelops my car, and I know I won't get that delicious fragrance out any time soon.

"It's scary how short life is," she speaks in a sobering tone, still looking directly through the window in front of us. "It's fragile, so easily broken." Her words have a slight slur, but she's keeping herself upright, her focus on the road ahead. I sneak glances over at her, taking in the sadness painted on her expression.

"Yes, I know." My answer is clipped, and I don't mean to be rude because I know why she's brought it up, but I'm not sure how to deal with my attraction to her. We're forbidden—by rules, by the place I work. And she's barely fucking legal. She's not mine to claim.

"My parents taught me to pray to God. They told me he's good and he'll keep me safe always, and then, guess what he does? He takes the only person who ever loved me away." Her voice sounds so damn sad I have second thoughts about what I want, about the plan.

I cast a glance over at her and notice the tears that trickle from her eyes.

"I mean, my aunt loves me, but I'm not hers. She didn't give birth to me." A sob falls from her lips, and I want nothing more than to hold her, to tell her life goes on, but I can't. I don't.

After her breakdown, the silence that fills the car is stifling. Perhaps I should tell her I lost my father too. Maybe I can console her, but that would mean touching her, feeling her, and I can't do that. A man only has so much restraint, and right now, mine is flimsy with her so close.

I don't have to ask where she lives. I recall

her address from the folder Dawson left on my desk and find the house easily. It's smaller than mine, but it's not a place to be frowned upon. Sitting on six acres more or less of land, the gardens are vast. The three-level mansion is built in a modern style with open brick in a soft brown and cream-colored awnings. The windows are all lit up with a golden glow, and I wonder why her aunt needs something this big for just the two of them.

I pull to a stop outside the gate, then turn to Arabella. Her eyes are glassy, her lips swollen and pouty, which has my mind filling with illicit thoughts.

"Look, you're young, and I know how much it hurts to lose people you love, people you thought would always be around. But you must remember, they wouldn't want you throwing your life away." My words seem to hang in the air between us. Her eyes search my face from my eyes down to my lips, and each time she glances at my mouth, I notice how her pupils dilate. I want nothing more than to steal her mouth with mine. But I sit back, as far away from her as I possibly can in the car.

"Don't pretend to care after being such an asshole back at the party," she spits with fire blazing in every word. "I don't like fake people, smiling to my face and scowling at my back, and for the record, I don't want people treating me with kid gloves." Her eyes lock on mine. She watches me for a long while.

"I'm no gentleman, Arabella," I whisper, never dropping my gaze, holding hers hostage for a moment too long. I want her to look right into me. I want her to see the dark parts of me I know will scare her away.

"I don't run away as easily as other girls might, Mr. Donati," she informs me with a soft smile on her lips. They curve upward at the corners, and her eyes shine with a challenge that has me leaning forward. A gasp tumbles from those plump lips as they part with surprise at my actions.

I lift my hand, tangling my fingers through the long locks of her hair, feeling the softness of the golden tresses, and I grip them harshly. I earn myself another dick-jolting whimper.

"Don't tempt me, little deviant," I growl, low and feral, and she shivers at my words.

"This isn't a game. No matter how much you try, I won't allow you to run this show. And to be clear, I'm not always one for breaking rules, but with you, I might make an exception."

This time, only the corner of her mouth turns into a grin. Her tongue darts out, licking her lower lip, wetting it just like I want to. "I'm not afraid of men like you," she tells me. "I've seen my fair share of *bad men*, and they don't scare me."

"This is a dangerous game you're playing, Arabella," I warn her once more, wanting her to fear me. I need her to, or I'll end up doing something I really shouldn't be doing—claiming her lips with my own.

She leans forward, her mouth inches from mine, and I can practically taste her purity. "What if I wasn't playing a game?" she challenges, her hot breath caressing over my face, and my cock hardens in my slacks. The zipper causing pain in my crotch from just how fucking hard she's making me. I release her hair but grip her face between my thumb and forefinger, holding her close.

"A deviant with angel's wings," I muse.

"You have no idea what you're doing. Playing adult games, and you're only a nineteen-year-old girl. I was being nice giving you a lift home, but—"

"I thought you weren't nice. Make up your mind about what you want, Mr. Donati." She whispers my name with condescending sweetness. "Thank you for the lift. I'll see you in class on Monday." She tugs free, pushing open the passenger door, and shutting it with a bang before sashaying toward the house. I watch her for a moment, how her hips sway, how her hair flicks left to right, and how those slender legs move.

I wait until she's inside the house, no doubt frustrated from our interaction. However, I'm anything but. I'm more turned on than I've been in a long fucking while. She thinks she can handle this game, but I'll make sure my little deviant works her ass off just to please me.

HER

THE PAST

I knew I shouldn't have done it, but I craved the attention, the touch of his fingertips as they trailed over my skin. In the darkness of the room, he wasn't him and I wasn't me. We were strangers, drenching ourselves in sin.

And I've never felt so good.

I said yes to him when I should've said no.

I don't at all regret it.

The door clicks, and I watch as he moves through the room. I don't breathe for a moment because I can't deny just how beautiful he is. Everything about him is perfect. From his broad shoulders to the finely chiseled dips and peaks of his torso.

My fingertips tingle to touch them. To feel his smooth skin under my hands. I want to trace my tongue along the V that snakes from his hips down into tight boxer briefs. I can't look away, committing him to memory because I know I'm not going to be here for long.

The thoughts in my mind swirl and spin. I should be at home, but I couldn't pass up the opportunity to see him once more. The door opens again, allowing light to stream through the bedroom, and she walks in. Long, dark hair cascading down her shoulders.

Jealousy burns through me, reminding me of the humanity that lies within me. The emotions that I usually push to the back of my mind. I don't like feeling these things, but he promised me it was us and nobody else.

They move together. His arms slip around her waist as she grips his shoulders, much like I did just last night. It's wrong. It's immoral. But the deviance I've become well acquainted with doesn't want to leave me be. So, instead of hiding it, I now bask in it.

They kiss, their mouths fuse, their tongues tangle, and his hands slip down to her ass. My clit throbs at the image before me. I want to touch myself just like he's touching her. His hands grip her *harshly, her whimpers can be heard from my spot at the window, and I can't stop my fingers from toying with my heated center through my panties and my yoga pants. I bite my lip to keep from moaning out loud.*

They fall to the bed where he fucked me last night, and between the desire and jealousy, my blood runs hot as they enjoy each other. I wait until he's inside her. I watch until she moans his name quietly.

And then I turn and run.

ARABELLA

Frustration ebbs and flows through me as I walk to school. I could've taken one of my aunt's cars, but I needed time to think. Saturday night in the car with Elian has replayed in my mind more times than I care to count. And even now as I make my way down the hill toward school, I can't stop thinking about his hand in my hair and how his hot breath fanned over my skin.

I won't admit how many times my hand snaked into my panties over the past couple of days. He's affected me. There's a dangerous allure to him that I want to play with, that I want to see come out.

Elian Donati may be forbidden, bad news all wrapped up in a perfectly tailored suit, but I do love a challenge. I was brought up in a world of lies and smiles, and I can play these so-called *adult* games as well as the next person.

I may be young, but I'm more mature than most of the girls my age. I'm about ten minutes from school when the rumble of a motorbike catches my attention. The sound slows to a stop beside me, and I turn to find Ahren grinning at me.

"Pretty girl," he says, tipping his fingers in a mock-salute greeting. "Can I offer you a ride?" His dark brow arches, and I want to admonish him for not wearing a helmet, but I realize he's holding it out to me. I take the item offered and slip it on. It's not far to school, but it would be nice to get there early.

I slide my leg over, settling in behind him, and he guns the engine, causing the vibration to slither up my legs, then my spine, all the way through every inch of me. Once my arms are wrapped around his waist, he pulls away, speeding down the road which leads to the school.

I wonder if Marleigh is with Alistor or if she's at school. After leaving the party, I didn't hear from her, even though I did send her a few text messages. I know she specifically went to the house for him, and I hope she's okay.

After Ahren pulls into a spot, he kills the engine and helps me off the bike. I pull off his helmet, handing it back to him before asking, "Do you know if Marleigh is okay?"

"Yeah," Ahren says with a chuckle. "She's been holed up in Alistor's bedroom all weekend. Probably can't walk straight at this point." His teasing tone makes me laugh.

"Ah, well that's sort of good, I guess."

Dark eyes lock on mine. It looks like he wants to say something, and I almost expect him to mention his brother, but he shakes his head. "I better get to work. How about you come hang out with me on Friday night?"

Hang out.

Friday night.

My usual party night. If I were back home.

"Is this a date? Or are you just being friendly?"

"Why can't it be both?" he asks, those dark eyes—that are nothing like his brother's—twinkle with mischief.

Nodding, I find myself agreeing. "I'd have to ask my aunt, but I don't see it being a problem as long as it's not a wild party." Ahren is gorgeous with boyish charm and a cocky wink. He looks at me with desire swirling in his gaze, and for a moment, I wonder if he'd be a better fit for me than Elian. He seems nice enough. Perhaps I should give him a chance.

"Great. I'll pick you up at six, and wear something comfortable." He trails those dark eyes over me from my head to my school skirt, which I've paired with knee-high black socks and shoes.

"I can do that," I tell him as I head toward the quad. "Oh … and thank you for the lift." I smile at him from over my shoulder, catching him looking at my ass. He doesn't come across as remorseful for his gawking when he shrugs and dons his helmet. Boys will be boys, I guess.

And for the first time since I arrived here, I truly believe Black Mountain may be good for me.

The first time I step into the library since I started at Black Mountain Academy I'm in awe. The room is massive, with windows that allow natural sunlight to stream into the space. There are rows and rows of books. Compared to my old school, this place is a sanctuary if ever I saw one.

Since I have a free hour, I grab a few history books for my paper and settle into a chair. Even though it's written, there are a few facts I want to recheck to make sure they're correct. I want to impress Elian, and even though he is an asshole, I want him to see that I'm competent and I deserve a good grade for the effort I put into my schoolwork.

If only he wasn't my history teacher. Having someone I loathe teach me my favorite subject is annoying as all hell. But what I decided yesterday was to put all my focus into getting straight As in his class. Then he'd have no reason to treat me like an immature little girl.

Losing myself in the books, I work on my paper, tweaking and changing dates that need to be amended. I don't notice anyone else in my space until a shadow crosses over me and I'm snapping my head up to find teal eyes locked on me.

"What are you doing here?"

The corner of his mouth ticks up into a wolfish grin. "I work here. I'm allowed to be in any room I please," he tells me with an air of confidence and superiority. Asshole. "Catching up on your homework?" His gaze snakes over my work.

"No. As a matter of fact, I finished my paper yesterday. I'm just making sure I have all the dates correct." My voice is a rushed whisper of frustration, and with the expression I get in response from Elian, I have a feeling he's enjoying my squirming.

"Then you have nothing to worry about," he tells me coolly. "I'll see you in a few minutes in my class, Ms. Davenport." He turns and walks away, leaving me glaring at his back. I don't know how this man can infuriate me so much. It's as if he's always looking at me like I'm about to fuck something up.

Granted, my past is dotted with a few bad choices, but that's where I've left them—in the past. I'm not that girl anymore. My aunt has given me a new lease on life, and I don't plan on repeating my mistakes.

I pack up the moment the bell rings and head out into the hallway into a crowd of students all rushing to their next class. As my footsteps click along the floor, I think about where I'm headed. Even though my paper is ready and I'm confident it's worthy of an A, maybe a B-plus, I have a feeling Elian is going to be harsher on grading mine than any of the other students.

When I reach his class, Melody is leaning over his desk, giggling at something she's just said, but those eyes, those iridescent pools of ocean blue, pierce me from over her shoulder, and I don't even think she noticed.

I can't say I'm jealous. I can't admit that at all. As I move through the classroom to my desk, I can feel his stare on me. It's as if we're magnets and he's attached himself to my soul. I have never been so flayed by someone by a mere glance.

I settle in my chair, catching his gaze the moment I look up, blue against steel. Once Melody leaves his desk, realizing she's no longer the object of his attention, I find myself trembling. Heat trails through me when Elian rises and moves to stand before us. Everything about this man has been perfected. From his broad shoulders to his tapered waist, and his chiseled features that would make any Greek god weep. Right down to the minute details, like even his shirt matches those endless pools of blue, and there's not a crease to be seen.

"Thank you all for joining me today," he says, his deep voice rumbling through each of us, affecting me more than I'd like. "I've gone through your papers on how you think history is relevant to modern society. I have to say I'm impressed at the level of interest and the way you all approached the subject."

A smile tilts his lips. It's slight, but it's there. I can't look away. As much as I know I should perhaps give Ahren a chance, I can't stop the attraction to his brother. Both Donati men seem to have a power over me, and I can't fight it.

But I don't want to be another giggly schoolgirl wanting her teacher, and I don't want to be another notch in Ahren's bedpost. It's not who I am. Elian turns to the blackboard, and I know it's time to focus on classwork rather than my raging teenage hormones. Sighing, I sit back and pick up my pencil. Time to take notes.

ARABELLA

The week has passed in a haze of classes and homework. Of papers and research, but I've enjoyed every moment. When I make my way downstairs, I find Aunt Midge sitting at the dining room table, poring through pages of documents.

"Hi," I greet, leaning in to press a kiss to her cheek.

"How's my favorite niece?" she asks, offering me a smile as she sits back and sets her pen down. The amount of paperwork looks daunting, but I settle in beside her.

"I'm good. A little nervous for this date."

"It's not some party you're going to is it?"

Shaking my head, I assure her, "No. Ahren

Donati is taking me out. We're just going for a drive. He's going to show me the town."

She watches me for a long while before nodding. "Fine. Be home at ten."

"I promise." I stand, smoothing down my pants before I glance at my phone. It's almost time for Ahren to pick me up, and I have to admit I'm nervous. I haven't been on a date in a long time. And I'm not sure what to expect with him. I promised myself I'm going to try to enjoy this evening and give Ahren a real chance. He's not Elian. But the more I mull it over in my mind, I realize the younger guy will be a better choice. For one, he's not my teacher, but also, he's closer to my age.

The rumble of the motorbike at the gate alerts me that he's arrived. Ahren kills the engine when he sees me, and he tugs off his helmet. Dark eyes lock on mine and a smile dances on his lips. "Hello, pretty girl," he greets me with a wink, which I must admit makes my stomach tumble with butterflies.

"Hi." I grab the offered helmet from Ahren and pull it on. Once I'm on the seat behind him with my arms wrapped around his torso, he pulls down the road. I can't deny the feel of his toned abs has me blushing. Each dip and peak under my fingertips sends heat sizzling through me. The warmth of him wrapping itself around me, and for a moment, I enjoy how we mold to each other.

The streets are quiet, making him go faster as we weave through the town and out onto a mountain track which winds toward what I'm guessing is the actual reason for the town's name.

We climb higher and higher, and my heart is pumping wildly in my chest. The speed, the freedom as the wind whips against me, everything about it is exhilarating. Ahren finally comes to a stop and kills the rumbling engine. He helps me off the bike before kicking out the stand.

"What are we doing up here?" I ask, but he shakes his head, placing an index finger over his full lips. He laces his fingers with mine as he leads me down a trail. "If you've brought me up here to kill me, you should know, I'm well versed in how to defend myself," I tell him with nervous energy drenched in every word.

"Ha," Ahren laughs out loud, the sound vibrating through his chest, deep and gravelly. "If I were going to kill someone, I wouldn't bring them anywhere near the town I live." We come to a deep ridge on the side of the mountain, and when I look out, I know why he brought me here.

The town is sprawled out with glittering yellow and gold lights. "This is incredible." I can tell exactly where the school is, and I can even make out where the party house is, Alistor's home. It's not the biggest town I've seen, I'm used to a city, but this is magical, just from where we're standing.

"I thought we could come up here and talk," Ahren says. When I glance over my shoulder, I find him staring at me. He knows—he must— that I like his brother. I'm sure it's obvious since I haven't really hidden it from anyone.

"Talk about what?"

"Come on." Ahren grins. "Are you going to deny you're into Elian?" he challenges, his dark eyes holding me hostage. I pray he can't really see the heat that burns on my cheeks because I'm certain they're bright red. "I thought so."

"He's my teacher. That's all there is to it. And it's against the rules even if I did."

"Rules are always meant to be broken," Ahren says, taking a step closer to me. He reaches for my face. Cupping my cheek in his palm, he swipes his thumb over my lower lip, and for a moment, I want to lean up on my tiptoes and just kiss him.

But I wait.

"And when rules are broken, they can be twisted until they suit you." His voice is merely a whisper. He leans in farther, and I don't move, because I want something real. I want to break the rules. "And I need to do this before I say anything more."

"Ahren …"

He crashes his mouth to mine, stealing my words and my breath. His tongue dances alongside mine, and his lips mold to my own. The kiss is gentle, and for a moment, I wonder if I'm doing the right thing. Ahren trails his hands over my shoulders, down my arms, and then he grips my hips.

He deepens the kiss, causing me to whimper, which only spurs him on. I tangle my hands around his neck, pulling him closer, craving the attention for a moment of unbidden lust. My body trembles when his hands grip my ass, and he lifts me against him, his body hard, ready for more, but he doesn't do anything other than kiss me.

I don't know how much time passes, but when Ahren breaks the kiss, there's a wolfish grin plastered on his face. "Now, when you kiss Elian, remember that we're nothing alike."

"What do you mean, *when* I kiss him?"

"Oh, trust me when I say he will kiss you," he tells me confidently. "I have no doubt about it." There's no amusement in his eyes, which only makes my heart thump in my chest.

"Then why did *you* kiss me?" I ask, confused at just what is happening here.

His eyes burn through me. "Because I wanted to know what your lips felt like. I wanted to know what you tasted like. And deep down, I wanted to steal something from him." His words are cryptic, and I want to ask him what he means, but he continues, "Also, I wanted to be the first kiss you had in this godforsaken town." Ahren is still holding onto me. He doesn't let me go when he presses a chaste kiss on my forehead.

"You make this sound like it's a terrible place to live," I muse as I stare up at him in the dusky light. As much as I like Ahren, I don't want to ping-pong between the two men.

"No. Not at all, but it's stifling. I don't like being in one place for too long. Elian doesn't mind it here." He shakes his head, lowering it so that our gazes are locked. "Tell me you didn't feel anything when I kissed you." There's a plea in his tone. He wants me to say I felt nothing, but that would be a lie.

"I can't tell you that," I admit honestly.

He smiles slowly. "Yeah, I thought so," he whispers, pulling me even closer. "I can see you like Elian. It's fine, I can live with that, but if you ever change your mind..." His words falter off into the darkness, leaving me to complete the sentence in my mind. "I'm sorry for making it seem as if I'm trying to one-up him, but I had to know if there was something more between us."

"I don't know. At this point, nothing is set in stone." And it's the truth. I do like Ahren. *What's not to like?* But I'm not sure what would happen if I did get a chance to be with Elian. I'm torn. I really am.

"Friends then?" His dark eyes dance with amusement, and I find myself nodding.

"How can I say no to you?" I slug him on the shoulder, earning me a groan.

Ahren leans in to whisper in my ear. "You can't. And I doubt you'd be able to say no to Elian either." Shaking my head, I try to find the answer in the myriad of scenarios that now dance in my mind, but I can't. He's right.

When Ahren looks at me again, I can tell there's a part of him that's disappointed. And I feel bad for doing it, but I couldn't be here with him while wondering what his brother is doing. "I'm sorry."

He shrugs it off as if it's nothing. "I'm used to him taking the lead. To be the first choice."

"What do you mean?" Confusion creases my forehead, bringing my brows together.

"Elian and I are foster brothers. I was adopted when I was five and grew up with him as my big brother. We don't tell anyone around town. It's not their business. But back when I was still living in Miami with him, we were vying for the same girl. We stupidly bet on who she would choose. I lost."

My mouth forms an O, and I struggle to school my expression. I never expected him to say that. "But you liked her more?" I ask, realizing he had his heart broken.

Ahren nods. "But it worked in my favor for one reason only. We have very similar taste in women," he adds with a wink.

"Oh my god, are you saying? Have you two ever …?"

"Yeah, a couple of times," he tells me as if he were reading my mind.

I know I must look like a fish, but my mouth drops open again, causing Ahren to chuckle at my reaction.

"I'm not saying you're into it, but …" He releases his hold on me and takes a step back, giving me space, and I'm thankful because I need it to process what he's telling me. "If you ever feel the need to be between us, let me know," he says as the corner of his mouth ticks upward.

"You mean? Both of you … would … I mean

…" My brows furrow, but I'm most certainly not confused. I'm taken back to *that* night. The one that ruined everything. I've experimented before, much to my dismay at how the story had been leaked to the press.

Ahren nods. "Yes."

"I don't know. I mean ..." Crossing my arms in front of my chest, I regard him through narrowed eyes, wondering if he knows about my past as wariness takes hold.

But then he continues, "Hey, don't knock it till you've tried it. That's my life's motto." He winks at me playfully, and I can't help but grin. Ahren has *bad boy* written all over him, and I know he'd make any girl happy. The thought of him *and* Elian wanting me does make my heart skip a few beats.

"Is that what you tell all the girls?" I tease, trying to steer away from *me* and more toward him and his past. Even though the thought of it makes my body ache, I push all those thoughts to the back of my mind and focus on the present moment.

"Nah, I just give them my pretty smile and they fall to their knees." He chuckles. "I mean, how can you say no to this?" His teasing eases the tension, and I can't help but laugh as well.

I roll my eyes. "Yeah, yeah." In an attempt to move the conversation, I ask, "Tell me about you, him, and your family. Since you know about my feelings for you and him, I'd like to know more about you both."

"Well, let's sit. I can tell you about me, but he needs to be the one to answer your questions about his life." He motions for the boulder that overlooks the city. Ahren helps me up and then hops onto the smooth stone beside me. "I lost my parents when I was a child. My mom worked for Elian's folks, and it was natural for them to take me in," he tells me, causing my head to snap in his direction.

"I'm so sorry."

"No need to be sorry. I grew up with a good family," he says, but he doesn't look at me. "It's one of those times when you want to feel sad, but they gave me something I never thought I'd have—a chance at a future. And then his dad …" His words taper off into nothing, the silence hanging heavy around us.

"His dad …?"

Ahren stares out across the vista, his jaw ticking as he grinds his teeth. Shit. I always put my foot in it. I shouldn't have asked, but I can't help wanting to know about him. And his brother.

"He was killed. That ain't my story to tell though."

"I'm sorry."

"I think it's best you talk to Elian about his folks." There's a sadness in his words. It's raw and painful. "He likes you. I haven't seen him so torn up about a woman before."

"I'm hardly a woman." I don't at all think I am. I'm nineteen, repeating my senior year, and I'm still reeling from the past. Being an adult is hard, and I wish I could be a little girl with my mom and dad making all my decisions.

"That's how we both see you. I think if he could swap places with me right now, he would," Ahren says, and that's when he glances over his shoulder at me.

"Why didn't he ask me then?" I question. It's whispered, but Ahren is sitting close to me, so I know he heard.

"My brother isn't the easiest person to

be around, and he thought I would be able to explain it better. I do like you, ever since I first saw you." There's a rawness in his words, a truth I wasn't expecting.

"Ahren, this is strange. I feel like I'm a pawn in a game being shifted back and forth over the chessboard. It's as if you're toying with me by kissing me and then expecting me to be okay with Elian wanting me." Even as I say the words, I wonder if I mean them. Because if I had to be honest, I did like kissing Ahren. He's the epitome of tall, dark, and handsome as well as being inked from shoulder to wrist, and I do like him. "I just … I don't know how this will work. I mean emotionally I'm already a mess."

This time, he chuckles, shaking his head as he loops his arm around my neck to pull me closer to him. "It's going to be okay," he tells me. "I'm sorry I kissed you. I really should've waited, perhaps explained before I did that. And I'm really sorry for being an asshole and just making you feel like you're some chess piece, because you're not." He presses a chaste kiss to my cheek. "I do like you. And so does Elian. You've told me you want him, which is fine. But I do want to be friends. I could be the big brother you never had."

"I'm not sure I can do this." My whisper gets lost in his shirt. I'm torn. My heart feels as if it's raging in a tug of war. One side I have Elian, and the other, I have Ahren. This isn't some one-night stand that's never going to hurt me. Perhaps I am growing up, because if this had happened a year ago, I would've jumped at the chance.

"You don't have to make any lasting decisions tonight." His voice is calm, cool, and it settles my erratic heartbeat with his words. "You can mull over your choices, think about it. I just needed you to know that I do like you, and I would love to get to know you, to learn who you are."

"You should've led with that." A small smile appears on my lips.

"I just needed you to know that I'm not trying to cheat my brother out of your affections, and he's not doing that to me," he admits, his eyes holding mine, keeping me entranced by his expression. "And if you did choose me, decide to try this" — he waves his hand between us

— "I can assure you that you'll never want for anything."

I nod. "And if I choose Elian?"

"It would be the same. Except, instead of waking up to brown eyes and a sexier body, you'd wake up to blue eyes and an older man." This makes us both laugh out loud. They are very different. But that's what makes them both so unique, so appealing.

"I need to wrap my head around it." I sigh. "I'm not ..." My words taper off into nothing because I'm at a loss for words. My past is dotted with mistakes. At nineteen, you'd think I'd been a lost cause.

"It's okay," Ahren says. Lacing his fingers through mine, he pulls my hand up to place a kiss on my knuckles. "It takes time to get used to the two of us." He doesn't say anything more, and we sit in silence watching the glittering lights of my new hometown sparkle before us.

I wonder as I sit there just how many other secrets are hidden within the walls of each and every house. And that causes me to ponder just what secrets lie within the walls of the Donati household that Ahren didn't want to talk about.

HIM

THE PRESENT

Excitement thrums through my veins. Knowing she's alone in her bedroom with those tiny shorts and tight little tank top that has my body alert. Thankfully, the darkness swallows me whole as I move closer to the window. Watching her has become my new pastime, a need that I quench every moment of the day.

I like the way she sways her hips, how her lips curve upward at the corners when she knows I'm watching. It's our game. The deviance simmers through our veins. And just because she's forbidden only makes me want her more.

The sleek, blonde hair that hangs like

shimmering gold has my fingers itching to tangle those strands, tugging her head back, and ensuring she's whimpering with need. I know how much she enjoys it. How she loves to feel me when I've lost all control.

When she reaches her bed, I can't stop my gaze from tracking her legs sliding under the covers. Her head falls to the pillow, and soon, her lashes flutter onto the apples of her cheeks.

Her window is bathed in darkness, but I see her. The silhouette of a woman. She's no longer a girl. Filling out just like I knew she would. I wonder if she dreams of me, of how roughly I'll pin her to the pretty princess bed and have my wicked way with her. My cock thickens when I think about it.

A soft moan filters through the sliver of the open window. Another follows shortly after, and that's when I notice just what her hand is doing. Smiling, I lock my gaze on her body as she writhes. A few seconds later, she flips over onto her stomach, and more whimpers fill my ears. She tugs the pillow, straddling it, and my hand grips my now rock-hard shaft, and I stroke myself through my pants. Her legs tremble as she rides the soft cushion, and I can't help but picture her doing the same thing to my cock.

I follow her movements. I crest along with her and come in my pants as she shudders and falls to the mattress. Soon, my little whore. So fucking soon.

ELIAN

My brother took it into his own hands to talk to Arabella. I gave him one night. One chance to see if there was anything between them. When he got back from the date Monday night, he didn't give much away. Only informing me that I'd won. A game of *his or mine*, and it seems I'm the victor.

Even though I wanted nothing more than to take her out, to sit and watch the stars with her, I knew it would be easier for my brother to do his thing, and if she chose him, then I'd be the better man and step aside. But I'm not because she does want me as much as I do her.

I convinced myself Ahren is better for her. He's much less of an asshole than I am, and I never once denied it. But knowing he kissed her, that's what's frustrating me more. I want my chance to make her see I want her. And I think it's time I did something about it.

It's not been easy with Arabella around. I'm distracted the moment she walks into my classroom. As much as I try to deny the attraction, it seems to have a hold on me. One I can't let go of.

The sun is streaming through the bedroom window. It's too early on a Saturday morning which reminds me we have two days apart. That will give her time to consider what Ahren told her, and when I see her on Monday, I can talk to her before class. The weekend is a reprieve of the frustration that ebbs and flows through me each time she's near.

I stare up at the ceiling, my focus on the patterns that hover over me. It's no use acting as if she's not real because even when we're apart, I still can't stop thinking about her. It's wrong, I should ask Dawson to send her to one of the other teachers, but each time I consider it, I don't act on it.

It's masochistic. But it also forces me to

admit that I'm alive, that I can feel. After I left the city, I promised myself to shut everything out. I had a job to do, and nothing was going to stand in my way, but then she walked into my classroom.

I reach for my phone on the nightstand. Unlocking it, I flip through the numbers, until I reach hers. It's meant to be used professionally. For emergencies at school or checking to see if she's okay if at any point she's not in class, but I find myself tapping out a message that has nothing to do with homework.

Elian: Are you spending the weekend reading or partying with your friend? E

After I hit send, I grin. Arabella may want to seem innocent, but I have a feeling there's a vixen under that sultry smirk and those pretty eyes. There's also a storm raging inside her, one that's attempting to come out and play. Which makes me want nothing more than to toy with her until she shows me who she really is.

I want to ask about her decision, but it's only been a few hours. I'm fucking nervous. It's ridiculous, but the tension twisting in my gut is tight, coiling, waiting for her to say yes or no. I have a feeling she'll agree to try it out, only because I know her. And she's got proclivities I never expected.

I've studied her file; I know everything there is to know about her. However, her past has nothing to do with why I'm testing her. I want to see how long it takes her to break, to admit she's playing a game. I want to wrap her around my finger, until she's begging for mercy. I want to see just how easily she'll obey. And when I get her down on her knees, I know I'll only want more. I've finally admitted I crave her more than I should, but I can't stop myself from toying with her.

She won't find herself in the same trouble she landed in back in the city. I'll be here, right beside her to keep her in line, along with Ahren. But I do want to test that iron will she seems to possess. My phone vibrates, and I pick it up, only for a smile to curl on my lips.

Arabella: Why? Would you like to join me? Or are you just checking up on me because you like me?

She's feisty. And I love it. I tap back my response and hit send.

Elian: I'd like to make sure you're safe. I may not be a nice man, but there are times I consider myself a level-headed adult.

I don't have to wait long, because the moment it shows delivered, there are dots that dance along the bottom of the screen. I'm tense, holding onto my phone waiting for her message to come through. I haven't truly allowed myself to do anything as stupid as this for so many years.

I may not be *that* old, but sometimes, it feels like I'm in my forties. At thirty, I'm at times shocked that I don't do what I'm sure most men my age do—sleep around with pretty girls who taunt and tease.

Arabella: I wouldn't call you level-headed, perhaps more … grumpy and rude. And why would you care if I'm safe?

That's the million-dollar question, sunshine, I think to myself. She's only a student in my class, but I feel as if I'm invested in her. As if she's mine to keep safe, she's mine to look after. But it's purely instinct on my part. I'm not responsible for her, but I just seem to *want* to be.

Elian: I'm straightforward, not rude. I'm serious, not grumpy. I don't know why I want to keep you safe. Perhaps I'm also losing my mind.

The raw honesty in my words scrapes at the inside of my chest. It makes no sense, but I admit how I'm feeling. She's one of the only people in this world who will get any form of honest emotion out of me. The other being my brother.

Arabella: Is that a show of emotion on your part, Mr. Donati?

I don't know how to respond. If I say yes, she'll only think she's the one in control. And that's not how this plays out. I'm the one who will take control of this situation. If she wants to play this game with me, I'm the rule master, and she'll be the pawn.

Elian: Emotions are for people who feel something. I don't feel. I merely calculate, ensure that what I'm doing will have a positive outcome.

Arabella: And I'm guessing you're probably lying in bed, messaging me early on a Saturday morning instead of waking up beside a hot woman?

Elian: Who I wake up beside is none of your business.

Arabella: I beg to differ. Because I have a feeling you'd like to be waking up next to me, Mr. Donati. And don't deny it. I've seen how you look at me.

Her message has my body responding, and it has my cock hard. The thought of feeling her silky skin beneath my fingertips is racing through my mind. I can't help but picture her body bowing as an orgasm takes hold of her. I want to hear her sounds, listen to her beg for mercy, but I'll deliver none.

Arabella: Did I get that right?

I smile.

I tap out a response.

I hit send.

And then I turn my phone off before we can continue this all weekend. Because I know I could. Her fiery nature has me wanting to talk to her all day every day. She's mature beyond her nineteen years.

But for now, we'll stop the game.

ARABELLA

Monday freaking morning.

I didn't hear anything back from Elian after his message. I've been thinking about it, then rethinking about it, and then driving myself crazy. I've considered what he said. It's the only thing I've thought about all weekend. And even yesterday, as I wrote my paper for history, I couldn't shake the thought of seeing Elian in class today.

I didn't respond to his last message from Saturday morning. But I have read it over and over again, and each time I did, I tried to pick apart our text conversation. It's strange to even think it, let alone want it, but as I get dressed, I can't deny there is something appealing about having an older guy crush on me.

I pick up my phone and scroll to his message again. The only reason I do it is to light the fire that rages inside me.

Elian: Don't flatter yourself, sunshine. You may burn bright, but I'm not blinded by your rays.

I'm not sure why it got to me so much. Perhaps he did it because he wanted to annoy me. Maybe he enjoys seeing me squirm. But I plan to make sure he's the one who's barely holding onto his restraint when I walk into his class today.

As I pull on my skirt, I make sure it's as short as I can get away with at school. Then I slowly run the tights up my legs until they stop just under the hemline. The white button-up is paired with a bright red bra underneath, which shows off my B-cup breasts.

As soon as I step foot in history today, I'm going right to his desk, and I'm going to tell him exactly what I think of him. Frustration burns through me that we can't be together publicly, not yet anyway. I thought we were making headway with the texts, but then he disappeared, and he didn't say anything more.

Grabbing my hair tie, I get my long hair over my shoulder, and my fingers move swiftly, braiding the thick, shiny locks almost all the way to the tips before looping the tie a couple of times.

Slipping my feet into my black boots, I tie the laces before I grab my backpack, along with my phone and keys. Even though I usually leave my phone at home, I'm going to need it after school because the plan is not to come home but to go to the Donati house with Ahren.

I can't stop smiling. For the first time in a while, I'm excited to go to class. I want to see him, to see if he'll admit what his brother said.

The focus I had put on my loneliness has shifted. When we pulled into town two weeks ago, I didn't know anyone, and I didn't expect to have already kissed a boy, and I never in my life would've thought an offer like the one that's been posed to me would be on the table.

Even though I'm looking forward to talking to Elian like an equal, I can't deny that even over the weekend, there were moments my depression hit me. A silence in the house and not having Aunt Midge home ate away at me. But I put on some loud music and I did my homework.

I will have hard days. They're not going to suddenly disappear overnight. Even as the years pass, I know the heartache of losing my dad won't completely heal. But I've learned from mommy dearest how to hide my pain, and that's what I do. In public, we don't show pain. We don't cry. That's better left for the privacy of my bedroom. *She would be so proud,* I think, sarcasm dripping from each word.

Sighing, I make my way down the hall. The thought of seeing Elian and Ahren today has me skipping toward the staircase. I do feel like a girl with a crush.

The blue eyes that pierce me from across the class do something to me. The way he stares sets my body aflame. I want to challenge him, to push him out of that cage he's locked himself in and make him see that these games are nothing more than him trying to be the good guy. But by his own admission, he's not.

After talking to Ahren on Friday night, I'm on pins and needles to see how this arrangement will play out. Knowing that Elian Donati wants me has butterflies fluttering in my stomach.

I spent two days considering the pros and cons about heading into a relationship with a man forbidden because he's my teacher. It's not the first time I've been in a situation like this, and I guess I'm going to have to tell them everything about my past if I do this.

And that's what's bothering me more than anything.

I don't want them to judge me. But even as I think it, I know that things could always turn out worse than they were before. Shrugging my backpack on my shoulder, I'm pulling open the door to our house when Aunt Midge appears from her office.

"Darling," she says. "I hope you're enjoying being here. I know it's not easy coming from the city, but the small town is lovely once you get used to it." When she nears me, I can smell the faint stench of men's cologne on her. It's not overly noticeable, but I wonder briefly what she's been up to. Since I started school, she hasn't been around much, with work being her excuse.

Even though I know my aunt loves to travel and hates being in one place for too long, I thought since I moved here she'd be more open to spending time with me. Clearly, I was mistaken.

"It's been okay. I'm getting by," I tell her. "I've missed you." I lock my gaze on hers, praying she doesn't give me some excuse again, but she just pulls me into a hug. I'm not sure what the hell is going on with her, but my gut twists with worry. "Are you okay?"

"Yes, of course, I am." When she steps back, I try my hardest to pinpoint a lie in her gaze, but if it was there before, it's gone now, though her expression is filled with anxiety. "I'm going to have some friends over for dinner, so if you're going out, that would be fine," she tells me. "I don't mind if you go out. Black Mountain is safe, and I know the kids here are good."

Nodding, I offer her a smile. "Are you sure you're okay?" I ask her again.

Aunt Midge nods. "Yes, darling," she tells me more confidently this time. "I would tell you if anything was the matter. Now get to school. I don't want you to be late." She kisses my forehead in a show of affection I never got from my mother.

When I get to the gate of the estate, I find a bike rumbling, waiting for me, and on it, the man who's going to twist me around his finger. Ahren grins before pulling off the helmet and handing it to me. Thankfully, I put my hair in a plait this morning. I slip on the helmet and hop onto the back. My arms twine around his middle, and I can't stop my hands from feeling the rigid muscle under his loose-fitting tee.

"Hold on, pretty girl," he says before pealing down the road toward the academy.

HER

THE PAST

The brightness of the day shimmers in the clear, blue sky, and I bask in the warmth. Laughter and chatter surround me, but I keep my eyes closed. Knowing I'll be able to see him soon keeps me calm. It's stupid to crush on him, but I know he'll want me when he realizes I'm better for him than she is. I would never do the things to him that she does, and all he has to do is see it.

My skin prickles suddenly, and it's as if he's right here, touching me, running those long fingers over my bared skin. The bikini is sexy, with bright red strings that hold up the scraps of material covering my important bits.

When I glance to the side, I see him. He's dressed in a pair of blue shorts that hug tapered hips, and I lick my lips when I notice the chiseled V that's cut deep into his waistband. For an older man, he's deliciously tempting, so consider me Eve in the Garden of Eden and him the apple.

They settle onto their blankets as they laugh at something. A picnic basket I'm guessing holds tasty treats along with drinks that bubble beside them. One thing I have noticed is that he doesn't spare any expense when it comes to food. Even in his own home, while he's cooking dinner, there are items of only organic quality.

It's only been two months since I first laid eyes on him. The party pops into mind, and I recall just how his gaze burned into me. It was purely by accident, but the times after were on purpose.

He couldn't resist the pull of the forbidden, and now neither can I. Desire flits through me at the memory and how the warmth of his body against mine sent me spiraling out of control. I spun around in his arms, and when the music stopped, he didn't let go. He held on until it was the final moment.

But he had no idea who I was. Even that night, when he tried to call my name, he couldn't, because

I'd vanished like Cinderella on the night of the ball. I didn't leave a shoe behind, and I most certainly didn't think I'd be the one to find him.

But here we are.

He grins at her. But he doesn't lean in to kiss her, which I'm grateful for. They sit back, and I notice how his gaze is on the ocean instead of the woman beside him. She picks up a book, a romance novel I've already devoured on my Kindle, and she flips the pages open until she settles back.

They seem like the loving couple most times. But there are those moments I pick up on the animosity that lingers between them. I'm not sure why they may feel like that about each other, but it's there, thick and heavy.

I smile as I lie back on my towel and close my eyes. Time to catch some rays before I'm meeting a friend. Well, a friend with a multitude of benefits. But he knows, the moment he sinks into my body, it's a stranger I'm thinking of.

And it's him I'll get someday soon.

ELIAN

The familiar rumble gets louder with every passing second, and when it reaches the academy, everyone turns to see my brother pulling into a parking space. His passenger is holding onto him as if he were her lifeline. Annoyance grips me, its fingers cloying at my insides, but it's only when the passenger pulls the helmet off that my body grows cold with jealousy.

It's never happened to me before. Ahren and I have had our fun. We've also had our agreements, and no other woman has caused me to simmer with the need to possess her like Arabella does. And I don't know how I'm going to share her with him.

Perhaps it's time I spoke to Ahren and pulled out of this arrangement. Because if I had to be brutally honest with myself, with my brother, I don't think I can allow him to have her.

She climbs off the bike as if it's no bother her being with him. A smile lights up her face, making my chest ache with the need to see her smile like that at me. She hands him back the helmet before planting a kiss on his cheek, which only causes my hands to fist at my sides.

Ahren glances my way, tipping his head in greeting with his smile telling me he's doing this to rile me up. My decision is made—I don't want her with my brother. She can't be with him because he's bad for her. But then, *what does that make me?*

Arabella sashays her ass toward me, her eyes sparking with challenge when she reaches me. Her lips are once again glossy and shiny, and I'm tempted to swipe that sticky shit off and give her something to grin about.

"Good morning, Mr. Donati," she says in a syrupy-sweet voice. The look in her eyes turn my blood hot, my body molten. My hand itches to spank her perfectly rounded ass. She's toying with me when I'm meant to be the one in control.

I follow her. Keeping my distance, I ensure my eyes are on her every second as she makes her way through the throng of students and into homeroom where she has her first class. It's empty because there's still fifteen minutes before the bell rings.

"What are you doing?" I stop at the desk where she's set her backpack down. "I'm done dancing around this thing between us. You want this?" I question, my voice tight with tension. My muscles ache. They're wound so tight I'm sure they'll snap if she pushes me further.

"If I say yes, what exactly does that get me?" she asks, a sly grin making her full lips look like a temptation sent straight from hell. If I didn't know any better, I would be convinced she is the devil incarnate. A succubus here to suck the soul from me. "I like Ahren, and if you want to tell me who I can and can't be friends with, then perhaps this isn't going to work after all."

I lean over her, knowing we could get caught at any moment. Heat sizzles between us when I grip her neck with my fingers wrapping right around the slender column. "Listen to me right fucking now. This isn't ending here. I say when it's over."

"Do you?" Her challenge is clear. She knows she has taken the power.

I'll allow her that.

I can't keep fighting this.

Our banter is filled with sexual tension. She may be younger than me, but she most certainly is not immature when it comes to this thing between us. "Meet me in my classroom this afternoon."

"And if I don't?" Her brow arches, and I slowly trail my gaze over her face, dropping it to her chest where I can see the red bra cupping her perfect tits.

I release her, stepping back before I bite out, "Then we're done."

"I don't accept that." Arabella folds her arms across her chest, the tight white shirt of her uniform molding to her tits, which doesn't help the fact that my cock is slowly waking.

"Are you trying to tell me you want Ahren and not me?" I throw out my challenge, causing her cheeks to darken with a blush that has my palm tingling. "Or is it that you want us both?"

Her mouth falls open, plump shimmering lips forming an O that has my zipper tightening.

I read about her little fling not long after her father died. I scanned every piece of evidence I could, learning about her being caught between the two sons of a politician, her father's competition. But that's not what got her caught—it was the fucking video one of the guys posted on his social media that had her face plastered across the news. But I have a feeling that's not the whole story. I will get it out of her, one way or another.

They were all high, tripping on drugs that should've put her in the hospital. When I saw the state of her, I knew she believed her father was dead. And that brought her here, to hide from the press, to finish her schooling. She was put back a year, forced to repeat and finally complete her senior year.

However, she's the daughter of Davenport, which is the reason she's captured my attention. When I received a folder delivered anonymously, the truth had been in black and white. I already knew who she was, but with concrete evidence of her daddy dearest, I must make my choice—

kill her or fuck her.

"I'm sure he told you what I said," she sasses me. She knows she has surprised me with her fire, but what she doesn't know is that I'm going to talk to Ahren. I want her. I can't share her. When he and I first spoke about it, I was convinced it wouldn't bother me. But it does. Far too much.

"Is that your final answer, little deviant?" My brow arches in question, the words lingering between us before she pulls out a strawberry lollipop she slowly unwraps before taking the ball-shaped sucker and popping it between her plump lips. "I know why you're here," I tell her, and for a split-second, I see the fear in her eyes. She knows what I'm talking about, but she shrugs it off. "And I will not allow you to fall into *that* dark rabbit hole again."

Arabella pulls the sticky candy from her mouth before asking, "Oh? And what do you think you know about me, Mr. Donati?" Her eyes say one thing, and her mouth says another. Those stormy grays shimmer with concern, with remorse, but those lips taunt me as if she's enjoying this immensely.

I step closer to her, ensuring there's no longer space between us. This is dangerous, being so close with the door open, but it only makes my dick harder. The thought of being seen, getting caught, and as her pupils dilate, I can see it turns her on as much as it does me.

I reach for her chin. Gripping it between my thumb and forefinger, I tip her head back, ensuring her pretty, steel gaze is locked on mine. "I think you want to stay back in my class after school. I want that too. Perhaps you should." I tip my head to the side and lean in farther. Not too close, but close enough so that only she hears my next words. "You'll shut the door behind you and come to my desk," I whisper, lowering my voice further. "And when you reach the wooden edge, you'll bend over it, sliding that tiny fucking skirt up and over your hips until your probably nonexistent panties are visible."

"What if—"

"Which means you'll be on display for me. I'll see your pretty pussy," I murmur in her face. Leaning in, I capture the lobe of her ear, biting down hard until I elicit the whimper I've been craving. Then I allow my lips to feather over her ear, and the scent of her perfume invades my senses. "And if you don't come to my class, the offer is off the table."

I turn and walk out of the room, leaving her alone to mull over my words. As much as I know I shouldn't be doing this, I can't stop myself from the ache that drives itself through my chest each time she walks into my class and every time she flits those heated orbs over me.

It's probably best that she doesn't obey me this afternoon. She should steer clear of me, run in the opposite direction, but something tells me Arabella is not thinking clearly, just like me. By the time I reach my classroom, I find the students already seated, waiting. I'm frazzled. No woman, or girl, has ever had my mind so fucked before, and I'm not sure how to handle it.

However, instead of thinking about her anymore, I flip open the textbook and get into the lesson I planned for today.

She won't come to the class.

She won't come to the class.

This is my mantra as I teach. And even though I continue silently replaying it in my mind, I know for a fact it's a lie.

I glance at the time. It's almost three, and I have to admit to myself, I'm nervous. A shadow at the threshold of my class has me whipping my head to the side, but I see Principal Dawson standing there.

"Good afternoon, Elian," he says in a serious tone. "I wanted to chat with you about the new student, Arabella Davenport." He steps deeper into the room, and my chest tightens at the mention of her name.

"Yes, of course. How can I help you?"

"I just wanted to get your feedback on how you think she's doing. I saw Arabella with your brother this morning."

For a moment, I'm stumped that Dawson would question me, but then again, I don't know if he's just being a good principal, or if there's more to it. He is the only person who knows we're brothers. I've kept my personal life private. Perhaps he's truly concerned about our new student. "Yes, they've become friends over the past few days. I'm not sure why her aunt would be concerned."

"Arabella has been in trouble before as you read in her file, she's … somewhat of a loose cannon. I just wanted to make sure that she wasn't doing anything that could land her in the sheriff's office. She's eighteen now, so that would be a serious offense on her part."

I push to my feet, needing to defend her. As much as she taunts me, I am almost certain she's not doing anything stupid to get herself in trouble with the law. "I can talk to her," I tell him. "I actually have a meeting with her this afternoon." Lie. It's all lies. A meeting with her is nothing more than a way to see if our attraction is more than a game.

"Thank you," he says. "That would be good. Even if you were to say, take her under your wing. Keep an eye on her. She's a good girl. Her aunt is convinced she has potential. She just needs the right guidance."

"I would be happy to help," I tell him earnestly as the door creaks, and I see the pretty girl in question on the threshold of her doom. A smile tilts my lips as I take in her wide eyes that flit between the principal and me. "Come in,

Arabella," I call to her, waiting for her reaction.

For a second, she seems tentative, but swallows it back and strolls inside with confidence in every stride. She stops at my desk, her eyes on mine.

"Hello, sir. Hello, Mr. Dawson," she greets us both, the wobble in her voice the only evidence that she's unsure of what my plan for her is. I told her to come in here, bend over my desk, and pull her skirt up, but with Dawson here, she seems far too wary.

"I will let you both get to your meeting. Arabella, as always, it's lovely to see you." Dawson shakes my hand before he disappears, and I'm left with my pretty sunshine.

"You can close the door," I tell her, gesturing with my chin toward it. Arabella stares at me for a moment before she turns and strides over to the exit. With a soft click, we're alone. The silence is deafening as we stand at a safe distance.

Arabella turns to me, her eyes tracking me like a huntress stalking her prey. When she reaches my gaze, she smiles. "I thought you and Ahren were into threesomes or some shit," she tells me. The girl has fire, and I'm determined to get burned.

"When you're here, alone with me, you will obey me," I respond, ignoring her comment. "Are you ready to play this game?"

"Illicit games with Mr. Donati," she muses, tapping her index finger on her plump, glossy lips. "Let me think about it."

"There's nothing to think about. The moment you accepted my offer was when you walked through that door," I say. "And you know for a fact you want this."

Amusement dances in her eyes. "I can't deny that I'm attracted to you," she acquiesces. "But then, do you really want me? Or am I just a distraction from your boring teacher life?"

"Why don't you pull that skirt up and show me what you want me to take and then we'll find out?" I tip my chin toward my desk with a grin creasing my usually serious expression.

Arabella strolls toward me, stopping inches away. "What are the rules of the game?" she whispers along my lips, which sends hot lava trickling through me.

I reach up with both hands, one grabbing her ponytail, the other her hip, and I tug her against me, forcing a gasp to tumble from that glossy mouth.

Wrong.

This is wrong.

But fuck it, she wants me. I'll give her everything she desires.

ARABELLA

"This is a secret. While you're my student, nobody can know about us," he tells me.

"A dirty secret," I test him, feeling every hard inch of him pressed against me. "Perhaps you should tell me more about what this entails," I whisper as I feel him throb. I can feel the warmth of him on my front, his lips a hair's breadth from mine. I want him to kiss me. I want to get lost in him.

He releases my hair when he tugs the tie and undoes the braid, allowing my golden locks to fall to the middle of my back. I may look the innocent angel, but I'm far from it. The polar opposite actually. There's a slight hint of a smile that graces his full lips. The ache I had the moment I laid eyes on him is back.

He lifts his hand, slow and meticulous. "Such pretty golden hair," he says. "Like the sun."

"What if I'm not the sun? What if I'm the moon? I only shine in the darkness," I challenge with a whispered plea for him to do more than just tangle a lock of hair around his finger.

"Before I read your file, I may have disagreed," he says. "But I believe you do glow within the murkiness that surrounds you." I've always felt more at ease in the dark. The bright lights have been blinding all my life. My father, a senator, and my mother, his secretary, were always watched. Bodyguards and media, along with the people who believed in my father. I grew up with the proverbial silver spoon, and I only spat it out the night it all came crashing down.

Stupidity took me to that party, and my choices ensured I was caught. But right now, I once again fight this raging war where one part of me is screaming for me to walk away from Elian Donati and never look back. But it's the other part, that dark, sinister corner of my soul that eases itself out of its cage, tentatively wanting to play with him.

"Did you enjoy your date with Ahren?" he asks, his voice a low rasp which gently scrapes along my skin, causing goosebumps to rise in the wake of his words.

"He kissed me. He put his lips on mine, and I liked it." The honesty doesn't burn my throat like it usually would. But I see the jealousy burning in Elian's eyes. Perhaps it's anger at the fact that I kissed his brother before him, or maybe it's envy that I enjoyed it.

I almost expect him to do something more, touch me where I ache and roughly plant his lips on mine, but he doesn't. The controlled yet barely restrained man releases me and sits back in his chair before gifting me a smile. A grin so dark and sinister something cold races up and down my spine as he regards me.

"Then choose," he finally speaks. "You decide here and now who you want, and it will happen." His command is no-nonsense. My heart skitters in my chest, thumping against my ribs in a timely beat of nervous energy.

"Are you serious?"

"Do I look like I'm joking, little deviant?" A dark brow arches, the corner of his mouth quirks. There is no longer a playful expression on his face. He's being utterly fucking serious. Slowly, he pulls out his phone. I watch him tap the screen and then he sets the device on the desk. The speaker is on because I can hear the ringing.

"Brother," Ahren's voice comes across the line. "What's up?"

"I have Ms. Davenport in my classroom right now," Elian speaks. "She's considering her choice. You or me."

"What are you talking about?" Ahren's clearly confused. I don't think his brother has told him about the change of plans. And I have a feeling Ahren's not happy about it. A smile graces Elian's perfect lips, and I wonder how it would feel to kiss him.

Would he be rough and commanding? Or gentle and seductive like Ahren?

"I'm offering Arabella a choice." Elian's voice is chilly. "It's up to her, you or me. And once she chooses, the other one steps back. Am I understood?"

"God, you can be a real dick sometimes," Ahren grumbles, but the shock in his expression is obvious. "Yeah, whatever, man," he tells his brother before he hangs up and we're listening to a silent line.

"There you go, Ms. Davenport," Elian says. "Make your choice." Cool, blue eyes hold me hostage. They're so clear, it's almost as if I can drown in them, just from his stare on me. He is beautiful. But I'm not going to submit to him like this.

"Ahren kissed me," I tell him. "I can only decide once you kiss me too." I fold my arms across my chest, jutting my hip out in an attempt to appear calm, but I'm nowhere near calm. My hands are trembling, but he can't see that because I tuck them away. I focus on keeping my legs straight, praying my knees don't give out.

Elian's lips form a perfectly salacious grin before he pushes to his feet and takes a step toward me. "You like being between us. Don't you?" he asks as he eats up the distance between us. *He knows.* The thought races through my mind, but I push it back. There's no way he could've found out about what happened. My father's team had those newspapers retract everything.

"I don't know what you mean."

He chuckles. His hands grip my hips, pulling me flush against him, and as much as I try to fight it, I can't because my body reacts to his. My stomach tumbles, and my heart leaps into my throat. I finally drop my hands at my sides, but I keep them fisted, hoping that the trembles will dissipate.

"You and Ahren were—"

My words are cut off the moment his mouth crashes against mine. Heat sears me from the softness and warmth of his lips. His fingers dig into my sides, causing me to whimper in pained pleasure. Elian takes it as his cue to slip his tongue into my mouth. He tastes me. It's commanding, his movements consume everything in my mind, and there's no longer an outside world. All that exists is him and me. And this fucking moment.

His hands trail over my hips and down to my ass. He holds me closer, and I can feel the ridge of him against my stomach. The warmth, the pulse, every hard inch. A low growl vibrates through his chest when I bite down on his tongue, sucking it into my mouth as if it were another part of his body.

I don't know how long we taunt each other, but by the time Elian breaks the kiss, I'm breathless. His eyes have darkened, the pupils black as night as he regards me closely.

"Are you going to make your choice now?" he challenges as if he already knows I'm going to choose him. He's confident. I must admit, Ahren's kiss was nothing compared to his brother's, but I have to consider just how this will work even if I did choose Elian.

I came to school convinced I had time. And I'd be happy about it. But right now, I'm unsure. I like both brothers, but I have a feeling I might be more attracted to Elian than Ahren.

My heart is already torn in two.

My phone chimes loudly in the empty room, causing me to jump away from Elian's hands. When I pull out the device, I find his brother's name flashing on the screen.

"Answer it," he tells me, knowing who's calling.

I swipe my finger across the screen and place the phone at my ear. "Hello."

"Have you made your choice yet?" he asks, the deep gravel of his tone making me ache.

"No," I answer honestly. I need time. I said that before, when I knew about them both wanting me, but now that I have to choose, I'm uncertain. My gaze cuts to Elian's, the blue shimmering with need, and I know if Ahren were here, he'd be looking at me the same way.

The door clicks behind me, causing me to spin on my heel, and I find Ahren on the threshold of the classroom. His dark eyes finding me, he lowers his hand holding his phone.

"Then I guess I better be here for the decision," he says, shutting himself inside and making his way toward the desk. He stops beside me, his arm snaking around my waist. "Did my brother tell you that he was testing you for this?"

"What?" I glance over at Elian who's shaking his head slowly. He looks at his brother, anger dancing in those endless pools. "What is he talking about?" Even as I ask the question, I know what Ahren means. They both know about my past.

"I got your file when you joined my class. I read up on what happened, why you came to Black Mountain, and I know about your past," Elian tells me. He doesn't flinch when he speaks, and he doesn't look away from me, the honesty in what he's telling me shining in his stare. "I know about the night you were arrested. And I know about your... proclivities."

"So, you and your brother decided to toy with me?" The surprise is clear in my voice. I can't be overly angry; the story made the media frenzy follow me around as if I were a celebrity. But I have to own it. I'm not ashamed of that night, it was fun, but what I am remorseful for was the drugs that night of the break in. I never want to dive down that rabbit hole ever again.

"Yes, I did play with your emotions, as well as Ahren's," Elian finally answers, bringing me back to the present. "I wanted to see if you could be swayed."

"But he's feeling guilty and wants your forgiveness," Ahren finishes his brother's sentence. "I won't stand in your way, pretty girl," Ahren tells me. "This is your choice. And

I will respect it. As I said to you on Friday, all I ask is for a fair chance to be your friend, even if you choose Elian." I find his honesty refreshing. His dark eyes simmer with affection, and even though we haven't known each other that long, I'm almost certain he's going to play a huge part in my life.

I turn to his brother. "Do you enjoy fucking around with people's lives?" I ask Elian who's watching intently. As angry as I am right now, I don't walk out like I should. "Tell me something, and I want complete honesty."

"Anything." Elian waves his hand as if he's not bothered by everything that's transpired here today. "I will never lie to you."

"Tell me, why me? Of all the girls in your class, you chose me. And why hurt your brother like this?" The thought of choosing one brother over the other makes my chest ache. It may be stupid, but I do like Ahren.

"Because when I look at you, you're the only *woman* in my class I want to fuck so hard she doesn't remember her name the next day," Elian says with a nonchalant shrug. "Putting my job on the line for a woman is not something I take lightly. My brother is stronger than you can imagine. His *hurt* is only his ego. Nothing more. But my reason for doing what I did was to give you a chance with someone closer to your age, someone you can walk hand-in-hand down the street with. And I needed to know if this was merely a game to you."

"But that's not what she wants, Elian." Ahren steps closer to me. His hand landing gently on my shoulder, and I glance into his dark stare. "I have to head out," he tells me, then leans in to press his lips to my cheek. Before he pulls away, he whispers, "It's okay. I promise you; he will be good to you. Just remember, you hold all the power." He turns and heads for the door because he knows my choice before I voice it. "Brother." He tips his head toward Elian before shutting us in the classroom alone.

I turn my gaze to Elian who's watching me with those iridescent eyes. "I'm not here to play games, Mr. Donati."

"Neither am I," he tells me, closing the distance between us, and at full height, I have to tip my head back to look at him. "Now tell me honestly, since the choice is yours, who is it going to be?"

He stares at me for a long while. There can't be any doubt in his mind anymore. He knows it's him, but he wants to hear me say it. My heart thuds, beating in my ears, deafening me. I need to make a choice. Even though I know I want Elian more than anything, it's the trust and affection in Ahren's eyes that keep me from opening my mouth.

Elian is forbidden.

But I can break the rules once more.

Can't I?

AHREN

Shrugging on my leather jacket, I make my way down the driveway to my bike. The apartment I'm renting has everything I need, and it also offers me solace from the town that's always had its watchful eyes on me. I haven't spoken to my brother or Arabella since yesterday afternoon, so I'm not sure what happened after I left. He hasn't called me, so I figure they're getting to know each other more intimately.

My choice to step back and allow Elian to be with Arabella doesn't hurt me, but it does frustrate me because she's fucking gorgeous. I want nothing more than to devour her whole, but I know she likes him. And I'm not a homewrecker.

My cell phone vibrates in my pocket, and when I pull it out, I see the name of a man who's offered me a chance at a job when I leave school. He's one of the most talented tattoo artists out there, and if he wants me to be his apprentice, I'll jump at the chance.

"Hey," I answer, nerves already twisting my gut at the prospect of working for him full time once I've graduated.

"Ahren," his deep voice barrels over the line. "I'm in town, and I wanted to know if you'd be up for a session tomorrow. I have a new client coming in, and she's willing to let you do something small on her. Test the ink, so to speak," he tells me.

"Yeah, of course." I'm smiling from ear to ear, and I'm sure he can hear it. "Thanks, man. I look forward to it."

"If you have any ideas, sketch them up and we can show her. I'm sure she'll want something unique." The fact that he's allowing me to do this means a lot. Elian has always told me I will be able to live my dreams, to have the career I've always wanted, but even growing up in Miami with his family looking after me, I knew I had to make it on my own.

"Most definitely. I'll see you tomorrow," I tell Scar. We hang up, and I'm thinking about how fortunate I was to meet him. Back in Miami, I hung out at a small dive bar on the beach where the Fallen Saints MC would hang out. The Miami chapter allowed me to spend time with them, and when I met the guys from the Arizona chapter, I knew where my future was headed.

I haven't yet told Elian I will definitely be patching in, but I know soon I'm going to have to come clean. The more time I spent with the guys, the more I realized that's where I belong. When Scar told me that he had his own studio not far from Black Mountain, I asked him if I could pop in over a weekend to watch him work, to learn from him, and he agreed.

Even though he doesn't head out to Black Mountain often, he called me up a few days ago and told me he's coming to town on business. I don't know his full story, but from what I gather, it's not good. He once confided in me that he needed to find his own way, even if it was for a short time. And since he opened his own place, he's been doing well.

With excitement rushing my veins, I hop on my bike and speed down to the gate, which slides open, allowing me out onto the road. First things first, I need to get to school.

When I walk up to the front door of the house, it whooshes open, and Elian steps out onto the porch. He's dressed in casual slacks with a black tee that makes him look far younger than he is. But his gaze is haunted, worry creasing his expression.

"What's up your ass?" I chuckle as I reach him.

"I'm concerned. I don't know if this is a good idea or not, and Arabella will be here in thirty minutes," he tells me, looking me over. I've always seen Elian as confident, commanding in any situation, but I can imagine taking a risk to be with her can be stressful.

I stop in front of him, looking directly at his worried expression. "Brother," I say, "let's go inside and talk." I follow him in, and we head into the living room where he picks up the bourbon bottle and pours us both a shot.

I left Miami before he did. So, when Mr. Donati was shot, I was all the way over here in Black Mountain.

I remember the phone call. Elian's cold, rigid voice telling me the old man was dead. He didn't cry, never showed an ounce of emotion. We sat talking late into the night when we reminisced about Dad, but he never shed a tear. After a couple of days, I went home. I needed to be there for him.

And then he told me he was coming here, he bought a house in Black Mountain, and then, he shocked me by informing me he got a job teaching so he would be around if I needed him. He was hard on me since the day his dad told him I was officially a Donati. In name only, but it didn't matter. Elian took it to heart. Giving me shit for my clothes, for my grades, but I knew he was only doing it to look out for me, and I appreciated every moment of it. Even though we don't live together at the moment, he's still my big brother.

He sets my drink on the table before turning to face the back garden. His back is to me, but

I can tell from the way his shoulders tense he's either really angry or just nervous.

"I want her, Ahren," he admits but doesn't look my way. I knew he would say that.

I pick up my drink and take a gulp before I ask, "Did she give you her answer?"

He shakes his head. "We were at a standoff. I didn't want to do anything at school, so I told her to come here. It would be easier for us to talk openly. The rules—"

"Rules are meant to be broken," I remind him of something he told me when we were younger. He taught me how to bend them, how to twist them until I was comfortable and could get what I wanted. And I must admit, it was good growing up with him.

"These rules could cost me my job."

"A job you don't need." Once more, a reminder that he has more money than god, and if he wants her, why can't he have her? He finally turns to me, the blue in his eyes sparking with frustration. I can't help but grin. I've known Eli all my life, and this is new to him—having emotions, feelings, and actually admitting them.

"I tried to build a life without the bullshit of

what I did in my past." A stark reminder skitters down my spine, and I recall his ex. The woman he walked away from back in Miami. She was a fucking stunner.

"If you don't take a chance, you'll never know."

"Life doesn't wait for those who sit idly by," he counters. He knows I'm right. Any guy can step up and take her away from him. It doesn't matter how much women tell you they want you, there's always a hint of doubt that niggles at your gut.

"What is it about her?"

"She's … she's broken, just like we are." There's a rawness to his words. I don't know much about Arabella, we didn't go into too much detail about her past the other night, and I know Elian has learned more than he's told me.

"Are you trying to say your little angel isn't as innocent as you'd like?" Even though I laugh it off because I can't imagine her doing anything illegal, when Elian's blue stare locks on mine, I realize there's more to the story than I thought.

"Perhaps," is all he tells me before pouring another shot of bourbon and downing it in one swallow. If it weren't for Alistor waiting on me, I would spend more time here, delving into the life of the girl who's so clearly caught his attention, but I have to go.

"I want to know the rest when I get back." I set the glass down on the table before I step up to Elian. "I'm heading to Alistor's, but tomorrow, I need to know what the fuck is going on."

"It's not my story to divulge," he informs me with a shrug.

"Like fuck it isn't. If this girl is coming into your home, if you're going to be with her, I need to know what the fuck she's hiding." I don't know why I'm so angry. Perhaps it's time for me to look out for the man who's always been by my side looking out for me. Or maybe I'm just concerned that Elian isn't seeing straight.

"Her past wasn't easy."

"Is that an excuse you're making for her?" I challenge, waiting for him to deny me. But he doesn't. He merely stares at me as if I've just hit home. "What has she done?"

"I—" We're interrupted by the door knocker hitting the heavy wood in the entrance foyer, and I realize I'm not getting the answers I want now. Elian's gaze darts behind me, and I turn to find Arabella walking into the living room led by my foster brother's maid who comes in here once a week.

"Mr. Donati, your guest is here." The older woman nods and leaves us. My brother is such an idiot living in this place with a fucking maid. I mean, it's not like it's a massive mansion like some of them around town.

"Hi," Arabella says, a shy smile tilting her pretty, plump lips. Her mouth is the perfect mix of seductive and sensual.

"Pretty girl," I greet her. She's dressed in a deep red top that hugs her figure with a casual sweater over it, tight black yoga pants, and a pair of boots. It's a casual look, nothing about her screams *temptress*, but that's what makes her so dangerous. A wolf in sheep's clothing.

I'm stunned at how understated her outfit is, but she still looks like the most beautiful girl I've ever seen. I need to fight this strange need to look after her. She's not mine. I agreed we could be friends, and I need to abide by my promise.

"Hi, Ahren." She grins, and I can't help but notice how the apples of her cheeks pinken.

And for a brief moment, I wonder if she's remembering our kiss.

I turn to Elian, my gaze locked on his, hoping he sees the silent message there. *I need to know.* "I'll see you around," I tell him before making my way past Arabella who smells like a strawberry field in summer. Fuck me. No wonder Elian is so entranced. She's delicious.

But no woman is worth a shitstorm.

I'm almost certain the pretty girl with the stormy eyes is a torrent waiting to happen.

HIM

THE PRESENT

Darkness descends on the day, and I'm here with her. She's alone tonight again, and I wonder briefly if he'll come around. I know they're better suited, but I can't deny the pull I have toward her.

It's in the shadows I find my craving for her burns brightest. Isn't that what they say? You need the darkness to see the stars shining. Well she is that. A star—exquisite, unique, and utterly alluring. She moves her way through the house, the lights flickering on and off as she goes, and finally, she reaches her bedroom. The window overlooks the garden, and I have a bird's-eye view of her beauty as she slowly tugs the tank top over her head.

The moment her tits are bared, my cock stirs against my zipper. The jeans I'm wearing are tight, but they only get tighter with her movements. Cascading blonde hair falls like a silk fountain. My fingers itch and tingle with need to tug them harshly until she whimpers with need.

She pulls the long strands into a ponytail before she slips on an almost-see-through nightdress. What I love about her is that she leaves her light on. She doesn't realize her window is my work of art, my entertainment. She does cast a glance out into the dark garden, but she doesn't see me. But she can most certainly feel my eyes on her.

When the yellow glow of the bulb finally goes to sleep, that's when I silently slip through the darkness and make my way to the car. I wanted to stay, to wait until she's asleep, but I have things to do and places to be. But soon enough, I'll spend the night. I'll lie beside her and watch her lashes flutter as she dreams.

I don't know where this darkness inside me comes from, but it's there, clawing at my insides, and the pretty blonde has only made it worse. As if a monster had been let loose and I no longer have control over my actions.

It's a lie.

I'm in control.

But the rope is pulled taut, it's close to snapping, and what happens after is anyone's guess.

ARABELLA

"Sit," Elian tells me in a tight grunt. The table is filled with textbooks and papers. He was clearly working on our essays before I arrived. My gaze takes in each name, but I don't find mine. I'm guessing it's hidden in the piles. "I read your paper," he informs me, forcing my eyes to meet his.

I wasn't expecting him to talk about school. Yesterday in the class, he said to meet him here where we can talk openly. Perhaps he's slowly getting to why I'm really here.

I settle on the couch. The cool leather makes me shiver as I scoot back so I'm comfortable. I have a feeling I'm going to need to be for this conversation. "Is there something wrong with it?"

Elian walks over to the liquor cabinet, and for a moment, I think he's going to offer me something to drink, but he doesn't. Instead, he pours a glass of water and brings it to the table before setting it in front of me.

"I'm intrigued by your writing," he tells me. "You have a real talent for storytelling."

"Thank you." I'm still not sure why he's invited me here; he could've told me this in class. But instead of pointing that out, I pick up the glass of water and take a long sip.

"Granted, this could've been done in class, but I like having you all to myself," he tells me, causing the water to choke me, and I splutter all over myself.

"What?" I croak, my gaze snapping to his.

The amusement that creases his expression only annoys me. "I thought you'd like being all alone here with me." He waves his hand in the air, but he doesn't make a move to come closer to me. I'm thankful for that because I don't know how I would've dealt with his overwhelming masculine scent and that stupid handsome face near me.

"I still don't understand what I'm doing here talking about schoolwork?"

"The privacy allows us to talk about anything we want," he tells me nonchalantly as he settles in the chair to watch my gawking response. "I spoke to Dawson, and he asked me to keep an eye on you because you suffered a great loss. I think you're capable of an A in all your classes." Elian leans forward with his arms on his thighs. "So, I *think* you need some private tutoring because even though you're most certainly not a bad student, I would prefer taking a hands-on approach." The salacious grin on his face explains why I'm here and why we're talking about school. It's the only way we're going to keep this ... relationship ... a secret. "So, will you tell me your version of your story, or am I meant to believe what's written in your student file?"

"My dad died two days after he and my mom told me they're sending me out here. I was angry," I tell him honestly. "Granted, I was never the easiest teenager. I did stupid shit to garner their attention, but for them to send me away hurt more than I ever considered."

"All children are difficult or hard work. Parents aren't meant to send their kids away," he tells me earnestly. Pain flashes in his eyes, and I wonder if it's for me or if he's recalling something from his past.

"I lashed out. Did something I now regret. So, anything you *think* you're doing to help me," I inform him, pushing to my feet. "It's not needed. I'm just like every other student. No special treatment is needed, and as I said before, and I will say again, I don't expect to be treated with kid gloves."

"Sit." The one word is ice cold, piercing my chest with its finality. There is no room for debate from the look in his eyes, and as much as I want to fight him on it, I don't.

Sighing, I sit down, but I don't get comfortable. If this asshole thinks I'm some fragile little girl, he has another fucking thing coming.

"I would like to know more about you," he says. "The night with the two men, and they were men, in their early twenties. What did you feel when you had their hands all over you?" His voice drops an octave; it's gruff.

"Why do you want to know about that?" I challenge quickly. I don't like talking about what I did. The past is where it needs to be—behind me. And as much as I would like someone to confide in, Mr. Donati is not the person I want to be spilling all my ugly secrets to.

"Pretty girls who do bad things are my kryptonite." Elian's tone turns to a husky growl, and the deep rumble sends a tingle straight between my thighs.

"Handsome men who do sinful things are my poison," I counter, which earns me a sexy grin. "But what if I'm one of those bad girls who would most probably be very bad news for you?" I watch how his mouth tilts, how his perfectly full lips turn upward at the corners, and his eyes seem to glow with intrigue. "My addiction."

"I doubt that, little deviant," he says. "If I were to order you on your knees right this very second, tell you to spread your legs and settle your cunt on my shoe and rub it until you're a whimpering mess ... would you?"

The rumble of his tone turns dark, his eyes dim with a shadow, and the usually bright blue has turned into a deep, endless ocean. There is a promise in his voice, one that warns me once more to run, to turn for the door.

But I don't.

"Yes."

A groan is the response to my affirmation. He doesn't realize that I've waited for this. I've craved, ached, and tormented myself just to hear those filthy words come from his mouth. He doesn't know it, but I will make him see.

"Then do it," he grunts, a smirk curling his full lips as he watches me. His pupils dilate, making the darkness in his eyes even more prominent. Slowly, ever so fucking slowly, I lower myself to my knees. I don't move. Silence fills the air, it hangs heavily, a guillotine ready to drop, and I'll go willingly if this is the last moment I have. My chest tightens, the ache that's been following me for months is still there, but with Elian's eyes on me, it eases.

His head tips to the side. He doesn't say anything. Instead, he narrows his eyes as he looks at me. Taking me in, he slowly shakes his head, and I almost think he's about to send me home, but he doesn't.

"At first, I wanted to fight this bullshit attraction I have," he says, his words lowering to a near whisper. My breath catches at his admission, and I wait for him to say more, but I'm met with silence.

"And now?" I'm once again poking the sleeping bear. But I don't care anymore because I want this.

He pushes to his feet. He's tall, looming over me and the coffee table that's still strewn with papers. But he doesn't come toward me. Instead, he goes to the liquor cabinet, and I watch him pour a generous shot of amber liquid.

He brings the tumbler to his lips as he settles back in the chair. His stare does nothing to calm my rapid heartbeat. I don't know if I'll ever be able to calm down while I'm around Elian. Especially when we're alone. Especially while I'm on my knees, waiting for him to command me into action.

"Tell me something, Arabella," he says when he settles in his chair again. Blue eyes pierce me, holding me hostage. "Why are you here?" He rests his right ankle on his left knee and sits back into the cushions with his blue eyes piercing me.

"You asked me—"

"No. I mean, why are you kneeling in my living room?" he asks, tipping his glass toward me. "When you could be out with Ahren and his friends, or perhaps with some other young guy from the academy? Someone your own age."

"I don't want someone my own age," I tell him fiercely as conviction burns in my words, but Elian doesn't seem convinced.

He looks at me through narrowed eyes for a long while before he responds, "Perhaps that's the truth. Is your young heart aching for a father figure? Or is it that you just enjoy being bad? Tell me your story, little deviant?"

"I'm—"

"And don't bullshit me. I want the truth, or you leave my house and never return." His command is fierce, cold, just like the way he's glaring at me.

How do I tell my history teacher I want him to rip all my clothes off and do sinful things to me? It sounds stupid when I think it in my mind. I spoke a big game of being all grown up, but the way Elian is looking at me right now, I feel like the teenager with a crush that I truly am. *Will he send me home if I told him how much I'd love him to dominate me?*

"Shall I take a guess?" Elian asks, his dark brow arching in question, and I nod. "I think you're here because when you're close to me, when I look at you, it makes your pretty cunt wet. Your heart skips a beat whenever I call your name, and your body aches for my touch even though you have no clue what I can do to you." His words send heat to my cheeks, and my body does respond in just the way he's mentioned. My heartbeat is deafening while my throat is thick with nervousness. My fingers tremble, and I know he can see my reaction to him.

He lifts a tumbler to his lips and takes a long sip, but he doesn't break eye contact, and I can't find words to refute his admission. Instead, I stay quiet because even if I wanted to, I can't deny he's right. Everything he's said, is exactly how I feel.

"And you're here because you think I might want to seal your lips with mine, perhaps even trail my hand over your shoulder, teasing my way down your arm until I grip your hip and tug you closer to me. Those are all gentle, affectionate movements. Things a good man might do."

The more he speaks, the deeper his voice gets. I can't stop myself from squirming as my ass rests on the heels of my feet, and those blue eyes track my movement. As infinitesimal as it is, Elian sees it all. He doesn't move; he doesn't even smile this time. The serious expression on his face is hard as stone, as if no emotions are taking hold of him the way they are of me.

"What would you do?" I keep my gaze locked on his. I don't want him to see me as weak because I'm not. I need him to look at the woman I am, not the girl. I'm old enough, and he knows it. The only thing keeping him at a distance is his job, which looking at his house, he doesn't need.

"I'm very restrained," he tells me. "I can wait this out until you finally admit how you feel. Let me make something very clear, Arabella," he says, then leans forward. His elbows on his knees, his left hand holding onto the tumbler, and his other hand taunting me as he snakes it through his dark hair. "You will admit it. I love to fuck, and I do it very dirty. I like to toy with the women I'm with. I show no mercy. Is that something you want? Because the moment you say yes, there is no turning back."

He gulps down the last of his bourbon before setting the glass on the folders on the table. The silence that awaits me is stifling. I need to answer him.

Can I do this? Can I be with him and still keep a shred of my dignity?

"I want to tell you, but …" My words taper off into the space between us, and it feels like my tongue is swollen and I can't speak. I want to tell him how much I crave everything he's saying, but for the first time in a long while, I'm scared.

"You have to understand something, Arabella. My job is something I can do without. But if we do this, if you can admit you want me and what I'm offering, then I'm not quitting. And you know why?" he asks. I shake my head *no.* "Because it's going to be much more fun fucking with you at school, right under all their noses. I'm going to bend you over my desk and spread those pretty thighs, and I'm going to make you come all over my cock right in the history class."

My body is flaming with desire. Lust courses through me like lava, hot and fiery. My cheeks burn bright, and I'm almost certain they're red. My panties are wet. The image of him doing just that causes my clit to throb painfully. I need the friction. Low in my belly, the ache starts. It twists and snarls and reminds me that all it would take is a featherlight touch to set me off.

I lock my gaze with his before I say, "I want this." Three words. One promise that I'm nervous about, but I can't take it back. I don't want to take it back.

Elian's dark brow arches, his eyes holding me hostage as he regards me. "You agree that you're mine to do with as I please?"

"Yes."

"You also agree that anything I say you will obey without debate?" The challenge in his gaze causes me to pause. Elian chuckles. "It's the only way you get me. I make the rules, you obey. I'm an extremely dominant man, and I like things done a certain way."

"What about Ahren?" I ask, realizing that he could ask me to be with them both, and even though I wouldn't possibly say no, I need to know where he stands on it.

"If you agree you're mine, my brother is off limits. Your friendship is all you'll have with him. I may have shared women with him in the past, but ..." Elian pushes to his feet, gifting me the view of his tall frame, causing my breath to catch in my throat. He doesn't move for a few moments, and I hungrily take him in as he smirks down at me. He slowly makes his way over to me, each step calculated, as if he knows the effect he has on me. He stops inches from where I'm kneeling, my face right at his crotch. He reaches for my chin. His cold, strong fingers grip me, controlling my movement as he tips my head back, ensuring we're eye to eye. "You're mine. And I'm not willing to see you take his dick in any of your pretty holes. I will own every part of you."

I open my mouth, then shut it again. I look directly into those blue depths and nod. "Fine."

"Consent is everything to me, Arabella." There's a warning in his tone, and I nod once more. "Words. I want your words, your eyes, and every other part of you."

"I do want this. You. As much as I shouldn't." The honesty in my words scrapes at my throat. Usually, I'm confident and outspoken, but with him, I feel like a girl unsure of herself. His blue eyes shine with desire when I push to my feet. It's time to take my power back. I'm the one who has all the say here. If I refuse, he can't do shit to me. "And I think as much as you try to be the *good teacher*, you're as needy as I am." My words spark him to life.

He grabs my arm, and I stumble into his body. Elian moves, his hands gripping my hips, and he tugs me close, so close I can feel every hard dip and peak of his muscular chest. His stomach is flat, toned, and then there's his crotch, which is flush against my stomach. A ridge pokes at me, thick and unrelenting, and I can only imagine what it would feel like inside me.

"Then we'll play my game. When you come to my class on Monday, no panties under that pretty skirt. You'll seat yourself in the front row, opposite my desk." His voice is rough, husky with lust. "Am I understood?"

"Yes, sir." I smile when the pupils in those aqua depths dilate. The corner of his mouth ticks upward, and he leans in closer. I want his lips on mine, I want them now, so I make the choice and push to my tiptoes, causing our mouths to fuse. It's only for a second, but it's enough to know that what I feel right now and how I felt with Ahren are two completely different things.

His hand snakes its way to my stomach, then drops to the waistband of my yoga pants and cups my pussy over my panties. The heel of his hand presses against my clit, sending waves of pleasure coursing through me. A whimper falls free, and my lashes flutter as pleasure streaks through me.

"Go home. Do not touch this pretty pussy of mine unless I tell you to," he warns me before stepping back and releasing me. A shiver wracks my frame at the sudden chill of not having Elian right up against me.

"But—"

He pierces me with a glare. "I said go home, Arabella," he bites out as he rakes his fingers through his dark hair. The man is insufferable.

If I weren't so attracted to him, I would've told him to fuck right off, but I can't deny the pull.

"Fine. See you Monday," I grit out, moving to the door.

"I will be in touch tonight. Don't think I'm not watching, little deviant," he calls to me as I'm shutting the front door. I don't respond. I'm angry, turned on, and utterly frustrated. Once in the car Aunt Midge said I could use, I pull out down the drive and out onto the street.

The man is a complete dickhead.

But I want him more than anything.

HER

THE PAST

It's not the pain of having your heart broken that kills, it's the moment when you see them smile at someone else. Living in the same city, the same town, even the same fucking building is too much. I wish I could run away. I want to race from this building, from my home, and never look back.

The deviant in me beckons, it calls to me, telling me that what I crave is right. But I know it's not. I shouldn't want this as much as I do, but he's mine. I'll always have him, and he'll always have me.

The addiction to him came along with the need to watch his life play out in a series of unfortunate scenes because he's doing all the wrong things. He's with all the wrong people, but you can't tell someone they're wrong because they won't believe you.

Instead, you wait until it's time and watch as they learn for themselves just how stupid they've been. It's the waiting that causes anxiety to twist in my gut. The tightening, the pain, the way my lungs struggle with breath because I know just how wrong this is.

The light drizzle does nothing to dampen his smile or his handsome face. It doesn't deter from how he walks into the building like he owns it. Guilt weighs on me. It grips me in a feral hold, claws scratching at me, making me bleed. I deserve it.

I lift my feet up against the window. My scruffy sneakers are in dire need of replacement, but they're my favorite pair. I wore them the night we met, and I doubt I'll ever get rid of them. They're one of the only items I own that reminds me that night was real. The costume I wore is gone, and the mask that covered my face has long since been discarded.

But the memory has been forever burned in my mind.

ELIAN

I should have kept her with me today. To learn all there is to know about her, but I needed time to plan. This isn't going to be straightforward, and we need to be extremely careful with what we do and where we do it. Granted, my house is safest, but I want to see how much she can take before she begs for my dick to be inside her.

The sun is already low in the sky, streaming directly through the patio doors when I pick up my phone and hit dial on her number. I want to take things slow because I don't want to overwhelm her, but then again, that's not who I am.

"Hello?" Her sweet, tentative voice comes

across the line making every inch of my body tense. There's an innocence to her voice, almost as if she hasn't seen the realness the world has to offer.

"Have you been a good girl for me today?" I ask, settling on the sofa which overlooks the back garden. The grass is lush, a bright green illuminated with a golden glow from the sun.

"I have. I even did my homework and didn't think of you for one fleeting second," she sasses with confidence, which makes me grin.

"Oh, I'm sure you haven't. Can you tell me with all honesty that you've been in your bedroom, all alone, not thinking about how much I'd love to taste your sweet cunt?"

"You have a foul mouth."

"That's the way you like it," I tell her. "If you didn't, you would have hung up after telling me to fuck off. You would never have agreed to this if you didn't want it. And I assure you, you're going to love when I put my filthy mouth on you." It's a promise, a vow that I will not break.

"Perhaps. I promise not to fall in love with your filthy mouth since you seem to be so confident about it." Her voice lowers to a husky whisper when she speaks, which I'm almost certain she's doing on purpose. But I can't stop the chuckle that escapes at her words.

"Love? That word is not in my vocabulary. It's a wasted emotion that doesn't bring any form of happiness. It keeps you locked in a box, one the other person puts you in because that's what they expect of you. I don't like boxes," I inform her.

"That's a really sad way to look at the world," Arabella counters, her voice strong and confident, which only notches up my respect for her. "Love doesn't keep you restrained in any way. I believe that if you love someone, they're the ones who unlock your shackles holding you back. The person who loves you unconditionally will ensure you soar rather than fall."

"Then why do they say you *fall* in love? Falling isn't something that can be done safely. It's painful and violent. Also, there is no such thing as unconditional love," I tell her with the confidence of someone who's been hurt too many times. I thought I was in love before, I was convinced that I had my forever, until it fell apart right before my eyes.

"Of course, there is," she insists. "Unconditional love comes in any form—friendship, family—"

"If you love someone without restraint, without limitations, there is an underlying promise of never hurting them, but human nature assures us that we can and will hurt someone, even if we love them. Think about any relationship you've ever had, whether it's your parents, friends, or even a boyfriend." I spit the last word with venom, and I wonder what she would make of my reaction to her having someone in her life. Someone who could give her what I can't. But I continue, "Did they not hurt you in some way? As small as it was, they would've. And if they don't hurt you, they try to change you."

Silence greets me, and I know she's really considering what I've said. Most women would laugh it off or counter before they've even really thought about it, but that's where she's different. Arabella is nothing like the other women or girls I've come across. Perhaps it's because of her upbringing. Maybe it's because of her past, but she's mature beyond her eighteen years.

"Perhaps, but they tend to change you in a good way," she tells me.

"So, then you're agreeing with my statement that it's not an unconditional love?" Once more, I throw out a challenge while I enjoy our conversation.

"Not entirely no, but it can be. If someone accepts every part of you, then yes, it's most definitely unconditional. Like I said, it depends on the person you're with." I've not been this intrigued by a woman in a long while. And I don't see her as a teen, even though she is. No, right now, this is a grown woman who's got a mind of her own.

"And what about when that love fails?" I challenge as I close my eyes, only to picture her right now. I want to be the asshole who asks what she's wearing and if she's on her bed. I want to make her feel things she's only probably read about in books, but I also ache to ensure she experiences things she couldn't dream up.

"Love fails when the two people in the relationship no longer deem it important. If you're with someone, you stay faithful. You open up about your darkest secrets and deepest fears." Her voice falls into the silence over the line, and I wish I could reach in and pull her out. I want her in my bed.

"I want to know what your darkest fantasies are," I tell her when she doesn't continue. "I want to know what makes your pretty cunt wet with need. What makes you touch yourself in the dead of night. That's how I'll learn your heart and mind, and that's how I'll figure out just how pure that soul of yours is."

"What makes you think it's pure?" she throws back easily, her voice firm. With every turn, she shocks me. She makes me question just who the fuck she is.

"I know it is because you haven't seen my darkness," I return easily.

Her breath stutters over the speaker, before she says, "Then show me." The challenge lingers between us, and my body turns hot, molten with the need to have her beneath me right fucking now.

I would say I'm too old for this shit, but I'm not. Far from it. I ponder her request for a moment before I drop my voice to a husky whisper and tell her, "Let's start this slow. What are you wearing?" It's the oldest line in the book, but it's going to show me if she's willing to take this seriously.

"My yoga pants and a tank top, which I might add are both extremely tight fitting." I can hear the amusement in her voice, which does nothing to calm my blood from simmering in my veins.

Ignoring the lightness in her words, I ask, "And underneath?"

For a few seconds, I'm met with silence before she tells me, "Black polka-dot panties with a matching bra." The image of her in those fucking scraps of material makes my cock thicken.

"Polka dots … Is that your favorite pattern?" I can't help but smirk.

"No, but these are so soft against my smooth skin." She's toying with me. The fact that she said smooth only earns her a growl from under my breath.

"Close your eyes and lie back on your bed or sofa, or even on the carpet." The order is nothing more than a murmur, but I know she heard me because I'm met with a soft whimper in response. I hear material shuffling, so I'm guessing she's moving to wherever she needs to be.

"Okay," Arabella's response is a slight moan.

"Good girl," I appraise her before continuing. "I want you to slide your hand over your neck. Allow your fingers to dance over your skin. A delicate flutter." Another moan is my only response. "Over your tank top and feel how your nipples harden under your touch. Now I want you to imagine that's my rough hand moving over your tits."

"Elian." She moans my name, causing my dick to leak with the need to be inside her. Or just to fucking see her, but the anonymity is fun … for now.

"I want you to take one nipple between your thumb and forefinger, and I want you to tweak it, gently at first." I know she's obeying me because her sensual sounds echo over the line toward me. "Now twist it hard. I want to hear you."

A stifled moan falls from her lips and finds its way through the speaker to me, which only makes my body rigid with the craving to feel her under me.

"Harder."

A scream, loud and clear, greets me.

"Good girl."

Fuck, this girl is a delicious distraction. Even though I shouldn't be doing this, I can't stop myself.

"I want you to slide that hand over your taut stomach, under those yoga pants, but not under your panties." There's silence this time, and I can't hear the path of her hand trailing to obey, but in my mind, I'm picturing her every move.

"Yes," she finally hisses in my ear.

"Press down on your clit. Make it tingle for me." I keep my voice a deep drawl, a murmur drenched with desire. "Circle it like you do late at night to those dark fantasies that run through your mind."

"Oh god." Arabella's voice drips with hunger, and I can't stop the smirk from curling my lips. "Elian."

"Are you all wet for me, little deviant?" I ask, knowing the answer, but I want to hear her say it. I want her to admit what she feels. My hand trails down to my crotch, my cock hard under my touch, and I squeeze, allowing the pain to send prickles of need down my spine.

"Please, let me come," she pleads in a soft whisper, which sets my body alight. I want my hand wrapped around her throat while I feel her cunt pulse around my dick.

Grinning, I respond, "No. Take your hand out of your pants right now."

"But—"

"Right. Fucking. Now." There's no argument because she knows if she doesn't obey, this is over. I made myself clear when I told her what I wanted. And she cannot refuse.

A frustrated sigh is her answer. "That was mean."

"I know. I'm not a nice man."

"Clearly," she sasses me, which makes me chuckle.

"At eight tonight, I want you to walk to the gate of your aunt's house. From there, you'll exit the property, turn left, and walk down to the stop sign before taking another left."

"That's going to take me toward the

mountain," she informs me like I don't know.

"Yes."

More silence before she asks, "But why would I do that?"

I can't help but smile at this girl's confidence. It's sexy. "You'll be wearing nothing but that tight little tank top and a pair of shorts. Nothing underneath. I'll be waiting for you a few yards down the trail."

"Okay." Her voice is light, agreeable, and I wonder if she's nervous. I want her to be trembling, and soon enough, she will be.

"I'll see you later, Arabella," I tell her before hanging up. Time to get everything I need to play up on that mountain with her. When I first moved to town, I explored every part of that place. Well, every part that's accessible. And I know all the hidden corners where I can enjoy her for a few hours.

Pushing to my feet, I head toward the hallway, right to the end of the east side of the house where my office is private from the rest of the home. Once inside, I inhale deeply. The scent of lavender hits my senses, calming me before I make my way to the desk. I open the laptop and click on the emails. It's time to set the wheels in motion.

I shouldn't be doing this, but I can't stop myself from wanting her. Hopefully, after a few evenings with the beauty, I'll be able to walk away. I need to get her out of my system because I'm playing a dangerous game.

I tap out the message with instructions which are precise, and I make it clear they must be followed or there will be consequences. Once I hit send, I make my way out of the office and lock the door.

The house is silent. It's nothing like the home I grew up in. I've always craved the quiet but never got it. Now that I can choose my own path, that's what I revel in.

But as I move through the house into the kitchen, I find myself wanting to hear her voice. Arabella's feisty words replay in my mind, her intelligent debate, her soft whisper. It's strange to think about someone like her in my life.

Most women have been a quick distraction from my mundane job, but with her … she's everywhere. And I'm going to make sure when I finally have her, I'm the only thing she'll ever fucking crave.

My little deviant.

ARABELLA

I can't believe I'm doing this. As I step out of the house, I shut the door behind me, hearing the click of the lock. I used to sneak out of the house when I was younger. At sixteen, I knew how to navigate our house without being found. Coming and going when I pleased. Even though I knew it was wrong, I did it anyway. Maybe if my Dad weren't gone, I would still be home and trying to make him proud. But I'm no longer his princess. I'm nothing more than a woman who's broken beyond repair. In my search for belonging, I'm going to meet my teacher in the dark.

As the wrought-iron gates slide closed, I glance around, noticing just how quiet this town is at night. Most people will probably be in their homes, or they'd be in town. The main strip has a movie theater and restaurants, boasting an array of cuisines. Thankfully, even though it's smaller than I'm used to, there are a number of things to keep people occupied.

I wonder briefly what it would look like in winter. With the snow thick on the ground and the trees bare from the cold weather. A shiver races up my spine as I make my way to the corner where I take a left.

I find the trail easy enough, and as promised, there's a car waiting for me. I notice the gleaming paint finish under the weak yellow light streaming down the entrance to the gravel road. The silver Aston Martin Vanquish is stunning with the license plate that reads Donati. It's different from the car he drove to the party, the night he drove me home, and I wonder just how many vehicles he owns.

Rolling my eyes, I step up to the passenger door and pull it open to find Elian sitting back, watching me slip into the seat. His blue eyes aren't as cold as they are in class. Now they're burning hot like an inferno raging through the forest.

"Hello, Mr. Donati," I greet, a smirk curling my lips in a playful gesture.

He takes me in, trailing his heated gaze from my head to my feet, then snapping back to my steel-gray eyes. "You look beautiful." His murmur is nothing more than a soft compliment, but I can't stop the blush from heating my cheeks.

"Thank you." I turn my attention to the front of the car before asking, "Where are we going?"

"A place I'd like to show you," Elian responds with a hint of amusement in his tone. "Did you enjoy our game earlier?" His question turns my body hot with a reminder of his words and just how much he turned me on with a mere phone call. I wonder briefly how it would feel if it was real. When I feel his words whisper along my neck, my cheek. "Arabella?"

"Yes, sorry." I glance at him, noticing how he grins at my shyness. This man does things to me I haven't ever experienced, and I don't even know him that well. "It was a new experience for me."

"You've never played over the phone?" The

shock in his voice makes me laugh.

I have to be honest with him. "No. Actually, I've only ever sent text messages, but nothing like what we did," I admit openly, wanting him to know this is a first for me, even though it's most probably not for him. I can't be jealous. We both have pasts, and I must live with the fact that I'm not going to be his first anything.

"Mm," he responds before pulling over and killing the engine. This time, he twists to look at me directly, and even in the dim light of the car, I can practically feel his eyes raking over me. "Tell me something," he starts. "What is it that you think we're doing here?"

I ponder his question, trying to figure out just what this is. I'm not sure because even though I know I want him, I'm still confused at how it will work. I'm not someone who can easily hide her feelings, that much is clear. And what we did earlier replays in my mind, reminding me that he can turn me inside out with just a few words.

"I don't know," I finally answer. "I wish I could tell you that this is normal, and I won't be one of those annoying girls who wants your attention, but …"

"But you have daddy issues," he finishes, causing me to snap my gaze toward him. The corner of his mouth tilts playfully, and for a moment, I consider slapping him and kissing him all at the same time. "I'm not judging," he tells me. "I'm the last person who should judge someone for their wants and needs."

"What are your wants and needs?" I ask, hoping to change the topic from me to him. I'm not comfortable delving into my psyche with him just yet.

Elian smiles, his eyes casting down toward the stereo instead of pinned on me like they usually are. "I like challenging the woman I'm with. I like pushing her boundaries and testing to see just how far she'd go to enjoy herself."

"Do I need a safe word for this?" My brows shoot up, my eyes wide as I regard him as he chuckles. The sound of his laugh is deep, and I wonder how it would feel if his chest were against mine.

"No, unless you'd like one." He lifts his gaze to meet mine. There's nothing in those blue orbs to scare me, but I can't help the shiver that takes hold of me. "What I did earlier, on the phone, that's only the tip of the iceberg," he informs me. "I like things … dangerous."

"Like?"

"Let's go for a walk," he tells me, pushing open the driver's door and exiting the vehicle. I follow suit and find him waiting at my side of the car with his proffered hand. I take it, lacing my fingers with his as he tugs me up the hill toward the same spot Ahren brought me to on our date. It seems like a lifetime ago because all I can think about is Elian.

The high trees cocoon us, swallowing us as we venture deeper into the woods surrounding the town and toward the bottom of the mountain.

"I have tracking on my phone," I joke as we take a left onto a path which snakes away from the ledge where I kissed Ahren.

"Good," he tells me. "At least you're being safe while being reckless," he teases. He doesn't stop, and our footfalls are the only sound on the detritus underfoot. When we finally come to a stop, Elian gestures with his hand toward a small cave sitting in the rock, which is only lit by the full silver moon above us.

"This is very remote." My remark is met with a chuckle.

"It is, but I thought we would need more privacy since we're not actually meant to be together late at night while you're wearing clothes that make my dick hard," he tells me nonchalantly, making my cheeks flame with embarrassment.

"You can't blame me for that," I sass him as we settle on a smooth rock ledge which is on the other side of where Ahren brought me, overlooking the opposite side of town. I didn't realize there was more to see, but from here, I can just make out the road that leads to Black Mountain. The heat of his shoulder and thigh warms me as we sit in silence for a long moment. I want to ask him so many questions—about his past, about his job, and his family, but I don't. Instead, I silently ponder just why I came out here tonight.

Ahren likes me, I know he does, and I could be with him right now. It would be so easy. I could walk around in public with him, hold his hand, and even kiss him, but instead, I chose a man who's against the rules.

"A penny for your thoughts," Elian says.

"I'm just wondering why I chose you," I tell him honestly. Even if I wanted to lie, it wouldn't make a difference because he needs to know what I'm thinking, or this won't work. I've seen too many relationships fall apart because of lies and secrets.

"Because you like a challenge. You like doing things that are against the rules." He doesn't sound surprised, and he doesn't even sound disappointed at my thoughts. "It makes sense. The forbidden is always that much sweeter," he tells me.

I have to agree. I've always been someone who enjoyed going against the grain. Even when I was a kid who didn't realize I was being bad. It started with little things, but by the time I turned sixteen, it became more. So much fucking more.

"Tell me about your family," Elian says suddenly.

"I grew up in the public eye. My father was a senator, as you know," I start my story. Even in the darkest night, I've never truly spoken about my life to anyone. "He loved me. I was

199

his little girl, which only pissed my mother off to no end. She would spend her days smiling like the dutiful wife, but at night, in our home, she was cold as ice."

"So, you didn't get along," he says. "Nothing new. Most kids have their favorite parent." There's a hint of sadness in Elian's tone, but I don't look at him because I don't want to stop him from talking, and I have a feeling if he felt my gaze on him, he'd shut himself off and turn to sex to cover up his heartbreak. "I learned all I know from my dad. Everything, including how to treat women. I watched his marriage break down. Before my mother divorced his cheating ass, she said one thing that always struck me as strange."

This time, I do look at him. "What was that?"

"Your son will never be like you," Elian responds, his voice thick with agony and pain.

"Why would she say that?"

"Because at the time, I was in love. I thought it was forever." My heart skips wildly in my chest at the thought of Elian with someone else, married to someone else. I can't explain it because I hardly know him, but I can't see him with another woman. For some reason, I just can't picture it, and it has nothing to do with jealousy.

"What happened?"

"She was the one to cheat on me. I was loyal. One thing my father always taught me, even though he didn't do it himself, was to be loyal to those around you." Elian looks straight ahead, his voice becoming nothing more than a pained whisper.

"Why would she cheat if—"

"I walked out one night after ..." Elian glances at me and offers a small smile. "Let's talk about you," he says. "Any serious boyfriends in your life?"

Shaking my head, I think back to my almost-limited experience. "No. Nothing serious. I ... I guess you could say I played around, learning, doing stupid shit." I shrug. "My father tried to keep me in line, but mostly I hated being home, so I would sneak out to parties and stay out all night with friends, with boys."

Elian stiffens beside me, his body rigid at my admission. He doesn't look at me when he asks, "Is it strange that makes me angry?" I don't know why I smile, but I do. I like that he's jealous because I don't feel like an idiot for my own emotions.

"Why me, Elian?" I ask something I questioned him about a while ago. I need to know if this is something real or only physical.

"I don't know, Arabella. All I can think about is pinning you down on the fucking ground right now and having my way with you." Elian's voice turns dark, the thick, huskiness tracing its way from my ear, all the way down between my legs.

"And then what?"

"Then I'll make you scream my name so loud everyone down there will hear you," he tells me, nudging his chin toward the endless view of the lights from the road that leads into town. "I want to feel your cunt around my dick. I want it to pulse and tighten, to stretch for me, and me only."

"That sounds like you're laying claim," I counter. The challenge in my voice is clear. "If this is going to be exclusive, then I want to know."

"Why? Because you want to go and fuck Ahren as well?" This time, Elian looks at me, his stare burning a hole right through my chest. There's a darkness in his voice.

I push to my feet, but before I can turn, hands grip my hips, and Elian pulls me onto his lap earning himself a squeal of surprise. His hold on me is fierce, and I can't move. His mouth is at my ear, hot breath fanning over it as he trails the tip of his tongue over the shell down to my neck.

He coos, "Tell me, little deviant. Want to fuck us both?" The dark tone that takes over his usually deep voice sends hot lava skittering through my veins.

"Why? Are you jealous if I did?"

His teeth sink into my neck, causing my body to shiver in his hold as he sucks the sensitive flesh into his mouth. "If you do this, like you agreed, you're mine, and mine only. I don't fucking share pussy with anyone." The command shudders through me, and those deep pools lock on me, holding me hostage.

Twisting around, just enough so he can see me, I focus on him, and notice his stare, but this time, it's burning hot and needy. "I'm not just a fuck-toy for you to use as you wish," I bite back, anger taking hold of me and making me rage at him. Elian arches a brow at me, amusement creasing his handsome features as he takes in my scowl.

"I didn't say anything of the sort," he tells me, trailing his hot touch down my thighs and slowly back up until he's reached the apex of my thighs. "And if you sit still like a good fucking girl," he speaks in a hush as his fingers dip under the material of my shorts until he finds what he's looking for. "Wet already."

"I've—"

"Been thinking about all the ways I can fuck you right here and now," he taunts as his index finger dips into me, not too far but far enough to have me trembling on his lap. "Are you also picturing how much I'm going to stretch this little hole?" His question is pure filth, and I can't stop the whimper that falls free from my lips.

He continues teasing me even though I haven't answered him. He inserts another finger into my heat, teasing me open. My hips buck of their own volition, and I'm lost to the world of pleasure as Elian takes me right to the edge.

My eyes flutter, my head drops back, and soon I'm lost to the euphoria trickling through me. A wave crests and then suddenly his hand is gone. His fingers are no longer inside me, and I'm shaking.

Snapping my gaze to his, I'm off his lap, practically stumbling backward as I glare at him. "What was that?" I croak, my throat thick with emotion as I almost feel like crying. For a moment, I think he's going to admit something to me, something I don't want to hear, but then he shakes his head and rises to his full height.

"I want you needy," he tells me. "I'm not a man who takes pleasure carelessly. The anticipation is what begs to be drawn out. The longer, the better."

Shaking my head, I huff. "That makes no sense. What's the point in prolonging the pain and living with it instead of just getting lost in the pleasure?" I may sound like a petulant child, but this is the third time he's left me hanging.

"Edging is part of the deal," he tells me nonchalantly. "You're welcome to walk away." His expression tells me he's not lying. He wouldn't care if I turned around and left him here. He wouldn't blink if I were to refuse him because he can get any woman he wants. And this may be stupid, but I'm the one who wants him.

"I never said I'm walking away. This is ridiculous though," I confess. "Can't I … I mean, I could touch myself." Even in my defiant words, there's a hint of uncertainty. Elian slowly lifts his hand, bringing his two fingers, the two that were inside me, and presses them to his tongue. A groan of pleasure rumbles in his chest. The sound is low and deep in his throat. And I watch as he sucks the wetness from both digits.

"If you even attempt to touch that gorgeously tight cunt and make those sweet juices flow, I'm going to make that ache that's swirling low in your belly so much worse." The threat hangs in the darkness, and this time, I do step up to him. I've waited, I've prayed and prayed, and now that I'm here, I can finally do something I've craved to do.

I lean up on my tiptoes and slowly press a kiss to the stubble on his angular jaw. The face that looks like it's been chiseled from the finest marble. Another feral sound comes from him, and the moment my tongue snakes out and teases the corner of his mouth, I get what I want.

His hands grip me harshly, his fingers dig into my upper arms, and he spins me around, slamming me against the smooth, cool rock where we'd been sitting. Shivers wrack my body, and he leans in close, his mouth inches from mine. I've been in control for the past few seconds, but it's not because I wanted to be. I was poking the proverbial sleeping bear. And he's woken up, baring his teeth.

"Don't think you can take me on," he whispers in my ear. "Because I'm not playing your game. We're playing mine." The heat of him cocoons me, but it's the hardness of his erection that turns me into a raging inferno. My cheeks burn with heat, and my body responds in a way I'd never felt before. Tilting my head, I meet those eyes that are no longer ice cold, but instead, they're a pure flame. "Feel that?" His hips roll, and I can't stop the nod because of course I can fucking feel it. The monster that will most probably break me open, split me in two, is currently nudged between us. "That's what you do to me, every fucking minute of the day."

In his eyes, I see why he's taunting me. It's to show me just how he feels when I'm near him in class, when he can't touch me. When we can't acknowledge each other outside of the protocol of teacher and student.

"Now, the next time, you think about touching yourself, remember this—" Elian thrusts against me "—is what I'm getting you ready for, and it will be when *I* think you're ready and not a moment sooner."

When he finally steps back, I'm left shivering and breathing hard. My panties were wet before, but now they're drenched. As much as I should run away from him—because I'm not sure I can take more teasing—I can't leave because I want him more than anything.

ELIAN

I took her home and did nothing more. I didn't kiss her goodnight, I didn't even touch her hand, but it feels as if she's been branded into me. She doesn't realize I know the darkest secret of all. I click open the email once more and stare at the screen. All the information I thought was true most definitely is. But she's nothing like I expected.

Arabella is turning me inside out. Even with the flavor of her silky skin on my tongue, I know this isn't going to be easy. The deal I made was concrete. I was convinced it would be smooth sailing, but this girl has made it clear she's not a pushover. And if I had to admit it, I'm enjoying our push and pull.

I'm losing my icy touch. My father would be so disappointed if he were still here. He taught me how to sniff out a rat, but this time, she blindsided me. The problem is, even though I'm dying to end this path in blood, just like the way it started, I'm not sure I can.

Leaning back, I close my eyes and bask in the silence, which is quickly broken by my phone ringing. I glance at my desk, a tumbler of whiskey sitting beside the noisy device. The name on screen is one I don't want to hear from, but I know if I don't answer it, I'll never hear the end of it.

"Hello," I say after swiping the screen.

"I'm here." Her voice comes through, clear and crisp.

My brows furrow in the dimly lit office. The red lights on my clock shout at me, telling me it's past midnight. "Why are you calling me?"

"I wanted to surprise you. I got in a few hours ago," she informs me as if we were planning on meeting. That's the last fucking thing I want.

"You're not making any sense." Pushing to my feet as awareness shakes me right down to the core, I move to the window to pull the curtain shut as if she's going to be standing on the other side of the door. Perhaps she is. This woman has *bunny boiler* tendencies.

"I'm in Black Mountain." Her voice is bright and airy, and I swear to god, my hand clenches the phone so hard I'm certain it's going to crack. *No. Fucking. Way.*

"Why are you here?" The question is bit out through clenched teeth. My jaw ticks, aching as I bite down hard to keep the rage from spilling into my response.

"I told you I wanted to see you," she tells me, but the moment she says it, one face pops into my mind, and it's not the one who I'm talking to. "I'll pass by the school tomorrow. I think a man who likes to play games will understand that you don't always win." The line dies, silence greets me, and before I have time to think, I'm lobbing the phone across the room. It lands on the thick carpet with a thud. A sigh leaves my lips when I realize this is a problem. A big fucking problem.

"Fuck!"

Picking up the landline, I dial Ahren's

number and wait for it. A few rings later, his voice comes through the line. "What's—"

"She's here," I grit out. My hands are still shaking with rage.

"What?" I can tell he's sleepy from the grogginess in his voice, but when it takes me a moment to answer, he interrupts my thoughts. "Oh fuck," Ahren mumbles as the noise of his bedding shifting comes through the line. "I'll be there in a few."

I hang up without answering him because I'm already deep in thought. I can't believe she is back, but showing her face at the school is against the rules we set out. If it weren't for the agreement Ahren and I came to with her, I would never have gotten the job at Black Mountain Academy. But now that she's here, I have a feeling nothing is going to stop her from telling everyone about last summer. When Ahren fucked her while I watched.

Usually, that wouldn't be a problem. I didn't enter her, and she was eighteen, but what I'm most worried about is that she knows there was a video. And I have a feeling she's here to get it back.

When I told Arabella I've done bad things, I wasn't lying. But I wasn't expecting the past to step right into my present and presumably fuck up my future. My phone rings once more, and I want to ignore it, but when I reach it as it beckons from the floor, I see Arabella's name, and I smile.

I. Fucking. Smile.

"Hi," I answer, keeping my voice low.

"Hi." She sounds as if she's about to pass out, but I can also hear the smile in her voice. "I wanted to see if you're still awake."

"So you called me after midnight?" I can't stop the banter. It's natural, nothing like I've experienced before.

"I figured if you weren't awake, being an old man and all, I would have left you a naughty voice message," she tells me with a giggle that's both seductive and sweet. Jesus, this girl is driving me up the fucking wall. I wasn't lying earlier when I told her my cock is always hard when she's around. It's true.

"Well then, what if I hang up and you call back?" I propose to her. "That way I can ignore your call and you can leave me that naughty message." The anger slowly dissipates as I listen to her laugh. It's boisterous, free, as if she's not got a care in this world. Perhaps she doesn't for this moment, and I settle in my chair and pray I can forget the rage that slowly took over me moments ago.

I know Ahren will be here soon, so I can't be long, but for a moment, I think about giving her what she needs.

"Are you needy for me?"

Her breath hitches at my question, and I smile. "Yes, I am."

My mouth tilts to her response. The breathy way she admits it only has my erection pressing against my zipper. "Good. Then I want you to take your index finger and slowly trace a line over your lips, top one, then lower one. And gently press your tongue to the bottom of your mouth. Imagine it's my thumb."

She doesn't respond, but her breathing is hard and fast.

"Then I want you to take that almost-wet finger and slide it over each nipple, slow and steady. Don't rush." My own hand moves to my crotch. I can't take my cock out, but I'll enjoy the tension that builds from just listening to her. "Then I want you to trail it down to your stomach, lower to your panties, and under that slinky material I'm sure you're wearing."

"What if I wasn't wearing panties?" Her challenge is clear. She's losing her inhibitions and allowing me in. Something I wanted since the first day of school.

"Then you're a bad girl, and when we're alone again, I'm going to punish you with my thick cock," I tell her, my tone feral and animalistic. "Now touch *my* pussy. Feel how wet you are just listening to my voice," I keep going. "Imagine me above you, looming over you, my hand over your mouth, keeping you quiet while you know it's wrong feeling like this about me."

"Elian." My name has added fuel to the already raging fire burning me from the inside out. "Please," she pleads, and my cock weeps. When I felt her tonight, how tight she is, and just how wet she got, I hadn't felt pain like that before. The agony of not feeling her around my dick in that moment took hold of me. It's fierce.

"Push two fingers inside, just like I did earlier," I command her. "Slowly pump them in and out. Imagine my tongue and fingers fucking you, getting you ready to take my dick in that pretty cunt."

"Oh, god, Elian," she moans, but over her sweet sounds, I hear the bike. It will be at least three minutes before he gets in here, so I turn my attention on her.

"Faster. Feel me, my hot breath in your ear, telling just how much I'm going to enjoy breaking you. I'm going to enjoy watching you swallow my dick, getting it all slobbery and wet before I slide into your tight hole. I want to feel you come and pulse around me, milking my dick."

"Fuck, Elian. Please, please let me come. I want it." More begging incites a grin on my face from ear to ear.

"I want your orgasms. All of them are mine. Am I understood?" The gruff tone of my voice has her whimpering on the line.

"Yes, yes, yours."

Her mumbling becomes incoherent and then I tell her, "Come. Imagine me deep inside that gorgeous little body, fucking my little deviant." That does it. She screams out loud, and I'm thankful she's alone at home. A second later, Ahren pushes open my office door and saunters inside as if he's not just gotten out of bed. "Good girl," I speak into the phone but glance at my brother.

My response is a chuckle, and he shakes his head. He settles on the chair opposite my desk after grabbing himself a drink and watches me from over the rim of the glass.

"Go to bed now," I tell her. "I'll call you in the morning."

"Thank you," Arabella says, and I can't stop my chest from tightening. "Goodnight," she tells me before hanging up, and I'm left staring at Ahren, the recollection of her first orgasm with me still fresh in my mind. But from the back, where I lock up all my bad memories, comes the reminder that *she's* back.

"So," Ahren speaks after swallowing a mouthful of the spiced rum I keep that's imported from Jamaica. "You're in a bit of shit."

"This needs to be squashed."

"She needs to learn that when you sign an agreement, you keep to it," Ahren informs me before tipping back the last drops of the rich,

217

honey-colored liquid and rises to get another. "You and Arabella are getting along well," he remarks but doesn't look at me.

"I need your help," I finally admit. I hate asking for help, even if it means I'll get something done sooner. I was brought up not to be weak, and the belief that asking for assistance in anything appears as if you're unable to do it, which in turn makes you weak.

"I know what to do."

I know he'll be good at it as well. Distraction is part of Ahren's DNA. The bad boy features and persona he's created keep women busy for days, weeks even. "Take her to the cabin," I suggest. "Give me a week. Let me just see where this thing between Arabella and I is going. If she's not to my liking, I can break it off." Even though it's a white lie I'm telling my brother, guilt still eats away at me.

"You know that your little stalker isn't going to stop," he tells me before settling back in the chair. "She'll come for you time and again because she believes she loves you. And," he says, tipping his glass toward me, "she thinks you love her."

"Pick her up tomorrow, take her on a ride, stop at the cabin, and then wait until it's late," I say. "There's a storm coming, if you can just keep her there for a few days at most." I don't like this, but it must be done. She came back when she was supposed to stay away. I can't have Arabella see her, talk to her, learn about who I really am. The little psycho was obsessed. I thought it was an innocent crush, one that would go away, but it became more. It turned dangerous.

Granted, she didn't tell Ahren, or he wouldn't be talking to me right now. But I have a feeling she'll most definitely tell Arabella, and that will only end in disaster.

"Fine." Ahren doesn't sound happy, but this needs to be done.

Just a few days.

That's all I need.

At least, that's what I tell myself.

HER

THE PAST

The darkness is where I'm best hidden. I watch him. This time it's a different woman. She's nothing like the last one. Anger surges through me. And I'm tempted to walk in there, to break his happy night apart. I picture it now. Me storming in to tell the whore to leave, and when I do, he'll hate-fuck me against the wall.

A smile spreads across my face when I think about it. He may send me away, but he can't deny that there's a connection between us. Even if he tries to fight it, I know he can't. He's trying to replace me with every woman in this fucking godforsaken town, and I hate it. Why can't he see just how perfect we are together?

I'll ensure he learns it soon. I've never wanted anyone like him, and the promise he made that night, to make me scream, to make me come all over his hands and cock, he still needs to make good on that.

The games he plays are hurtful, but he has to learn that when you toy with another person's emotions, there are repercussions. I grip the knife in my hand. The sleek steel is cold, and I enjoy the ache that comes with the hold I have on it.

A smile graces my lips as I think about watching her bleed out. The thought of her neck being slashed makes every part of my body tingle with happiness.

Soon, Elian.

Soon you'll be mine and nobody else's.

The moment I step foot in his class, I know I'm going to have a hard time not remembering what we did on the phone last night. Each day of coming to his class has been difficult because I know just how much I am liking him. He feeds my inner monster, the girl who craves what he can offer. Most women are too afraid to admit they enjoy the darker side of sex. And even at nineteen, I'm still ashamed at times. But with Elian, I feel free.

When I sit in the front row, the corners of his mouth kick up into a grin so salacious my stomach somersaults as I wonder just what's going through his head. Marleigh joins me, slipping in beside me.

"Hey, babe."

"Hey, gorge," Marleigh greets, grinning like she most probably just got laid. She must have because her cheeks are flushed and her lips are swollen. I wonder if Alistor was here, dropping her off. "What a night," she tells me, and I realize my suspicions are true.

When one of the boys from class steps up to the desk I'm sitting in, it's Elian who speaks up. "Allow Ms. Davenport to sit up front. She's

222

not overly focused on her work, and I'd like to keep an eye on her." His voice is tainted with amusement.

Embarrassment burns my cheeks as everyone in the class turns to look at me. I want the floor to swallow me whole right now. I can't believe he just said and did that. The amusement in his stare dances like flames in a gentle breeze. His mouth quirks into a sinful smirk, a challenge. He's waiting for me to retort, to say something I might regret later, but I'm not going to give him the benefit of seeing that.

"Right, class," he says as he turns to the board. There's an iPad set up on the side of his desk, and even though I'm sitting comfortably, I have a feeling I know why it's there. "Today, we're going to watch a movie," he tells us before connecting the device to a cable. With a remote in hand, he clicks on the projector, and we're soon in a dimly lit classroom.

"This is going to be a fun hour, so sit back and pay attention," Elian informs us as he takes a look around the class, but when he settles in for the show, I realize why he asked me to forego underwear. He sits on the tabletop, and as the movie starts, I can't tear my eyes away from him. But it's his gaze trailing down, all the way to my legs where I know he can see under the short black skirt.

I'm almost certain he can feel me looking at him. There's no doubt, but I can't drag my attention to the screen. It's an old, black-and-white movie I have no interest in seeing. After a moment, he turns his head, his eyes boring into me as he lifts his hand, placing his index finger on his lips, then, ever so slowly, his tongue peeks out, and the reminder of him tasting me hits me with full force.

Snapping my gaze toward the screen, I feel my cheeks burn as the moment replays in my mind. Characters on the screen move about, they talk, and they act their hearts out, but my focus is not at all on the storyline.

It's on my teacher.

The bell rings shrilly, shocking me out of my stupor, and the lights go on, blinding us all as the screen is turned off and we're shot back to reality. If you asked me what that was about, I couldn't tell you, because the whole hour was spent with the heat of Elian so close, yet so damn far.

"Arabella, can I see you before you leave?" Elian asks in a controlled, professional tone, and as the students file out, I pack my backpack and say my "see you later" to Marleigh before I head to Elian's desk.

He's working on papers, grading them with a dark-red marker. For a moment, I wonder why he's here. He could've been sitting at the pool, sipping a drink, not slaving over the students' essays. I have to ask him soon. I want to learn all there is to know about him, and I hope tonight we're able to talk.

"Is there a problem?"

"Tonight, at six, I want you at my house," he speaks as he circles a large red A on the white page. When he finally looks up, I grin, noticing how handsome he looks with glasses on. It's only for a few moments that he wears them, but it most definitely makes him hotter.

"Okay, I can do that."

He reaches for something under his desk before looking up at me. "Shower at home, and wear what's in that box under your clothes." His chin gestures to a box he sets on the desktop, one I noticed when I walked in peeking out from under his desk.

"What is that?"

"Open it when you get home." It's not an entirely large box, so I can only imagine what's inside. Lingerie, something tiny because nothing I would usually wear would fit in a box like this.

"Do you have any preference on what I wear? Clothing wise?"

"No." The word is curt, yet there's a hint of the desire I heard last night. "Because you won't be wearing it for very long after you walk into my home."

A small smile creeps on my face. "So, this is a date?" I know I shouldn't ask; he has made it clear that he only wants sex, and even though I'm fine with that, I can't stop myself from the wishful thinking that's taken over me.

Elian stops what he's doing to look up at me. His eyes lock on mine, and I almost expect him to scream and shout, but he shocks me by grinning.

"It could be," he says. "Who knows just

how much I'll do to have you on top of me?" he continues, which earns himself an eye roll from me. Just when I thought he was being nice. "I told you, I don't date, but let's not rule anything out. Okay?"

"Okay." I nod before taking the box, shouldering my backpack, and heading for the door. I stop on the threshold and glance at him, expecting him to be looking at his work, but instead, his stare is on me. "See you later." I keep my voice low since there are people outside the classroom.

I don't wait for a response. On the quad, Marleigh comes racing for me, and I know she's going to ask about him keeping me after class. Her eyes are shimmering with questions, her expression glinting with knowing.

"Oh my god, I can't believe you and teach," she hisses in my ear when we're far enough away from everyone else.

"Shh." I don't know why I'm shushing her because nobody heard, but just the thought of someone finding out scares the living crap out of me. I'm still nervous as my thoughts take me to tonight. I don't know just what he expects of me. I'm not even sure what's in the box, and the unknown is scarier than watching something unfold right before you.

"Are you seriously dating Donati?" Her voice is barely a whisper, but the question has me looking around, even though we've moved to the opposite side of the quad where nobody ever comes.

The problem with thinking you're safe is that usually you're not. I look at Marleigh who's practically salivating at the thought of Elian and me being a couple. *But what do I tell her?* No, we're just fucking. Even to my ears it sounds as if he's using me when I believe it's the other way around.

"We're not exactly dating," I finally admit. My chest clenches, my heart rate spiking when I see him walking down the steps toward the parking lot. He looks so good, and that's where the problem lies. Even though I know I'm a beautiful girl, deep down I still wonder why he chose me.

"Come on, you have to give me something?" Marleigh pleads just as Elian glances at us. He tips his head to the side, a small grin on his face, but it's not amusement. He's waiting for me to say something. He can't hear us, he's too far away, but I have a feeling he's going to read my lips.

"Nothing. There's honestly nothing going on," I tell her as I tear my gaze away from him. A lie. They're always lies. Everything in my life has been one lie after another.

"Well," she responds, completely oblivious to the fact that he's watching us. "If anything happens, I need to know. For research purposes," Marleigh tacks on playfully, causing me to laugh.

Elian walks off, slides into the driver's seat of a sleek, black Maserati I recognize. Only at a place like this do teachers drive million-dollar cars. I lock my gaze on my friend again and smile.

"You'll be the first to know."

It's a promise I can't keep, but I make it anyway. I'm getting myself into shit. Deep fucking shit, but the need that courses through me each time I'm near him is alarming. And I can't fight the desire I feel for him. Not anymore.

I want him, and I've learned that I can

always get what I want.

Even if it hurts me in the end.

ARABELLA

"You came," Elian says as if he wasn't expecting me. I'm not sure what I walked into, but tension hangs heavily in the air. I'm wearing the underwear he purchased for me, and the heightened anticipation that shimmies through me as I move makes me squirm.

I decided on a sleek black dress, which hangs to my feet and covers the beautiful lingerie set Elian wanted me to wear. The exquisite lace hugs my body. Panties that should be made illegal cup my pussy and cut along the cheeks of my ass. The bra is perfectly fitted against my breasts, and along the nipples are smooth pearls sewn delicately into the fabric that rub against my hardened buds with every move I make.

I smile. "You invited me," I remind him. My nerves have gotten the better of me, and as I tangle my fingers in front of me, I notice how those blue orbs spark as they take me in from head to toe. I haven't really looked at the living room, but under the scrutiny of Elian Donati, I cast my gaze over the room.

The furniture is all black suede, and a large fireplace sits against one wall opposite the couches. Silver illuminates the room as moonlight shimmers through the window, lighting the gray carpet, which is thick and looks so soft.

He doesn't say anything about my dress. Instead, he asks, "Would you like a drink?"

"I don't like the hard stuff. Anything light?" I reply with a grin on my face. I don't want to remind him that I'm barely nineteen, and I most definitely don't want him thinking about it when he takes this dress off. Because all that's racing through my mind is what his reaction will be when he sees the gift he bought for me.

"I have white wine, or you can have a vodka with juice?" he offers, a smirk forming on his lips, and I squirm at how he makes me feel. How his movements affect the butterflies in my stomach.

I can't help but smile. "Aren't you meant to be advising me *not* to drink?" I arch a brow as he turns to face me fully.

"Can I reform a little deviant like you?" Elian challenges with a quirk of his dark eyebrow. He regards me with amusement, and I take him in slowly, noting just how handsome he is.

Tipping my head to the side, I counter, "Do you want to?" There's something powerful about having a man look at me like he's doing right now. As if he wants to devour me, but he's holding onto a shred of restraint that makes my body tremble.

I'm almost sure seeing him lose control will be a site. Strong, brutal, and nearly violent. The idea makes my thighs clench. I'm challenging him, but it's impossible to stop myself. There's a seductiveness about Elian I like seeing when he looks at me.

"Make no mistake. You being here, my little deviant, doesn't mean you're in control. I'm the one who will hold your pleasure in my hands, and I'll enjoy watching you squirm under my touch." His gaze trails from my eyes, over my lips, down my chest, all the way to my feet before snapping back to my face.

He takes a few seemingly controlled steps toward me, meticulously calculated, so by the time he reaches me, I'm breathless, waiting for the monster to attack. Elian reaches up, his hand tangling in my hair, and with a gentle tug, a gasp falls from my lips when he leans in. His face is inches from mine, his warm breath fanning over my mouth, and for a moment, all I want is for him to kiss me. If I move, my lips will most certainly be against his, but just like the night in the car, he doesn't come closer.

"Now, would you like a drink?" he whispers, the words feathering themselves over me, causing goosebumps to rise on every inch of my skin.

"Yes, please." My murmur is nothing more than a tormented plea. The smirk that graces Elian's lips makes my stomach flip-flop wildly. He releases me, steps back, and leaves me in the living room without another word.

I turn to the room, making my way to the fireplace where I find three framed photos. One picture of a beach has Elian standing on the cream-colored sand grinning at whoever took the photo. He's in a pair of shorts and a tank top, so I can't see his body, but from the broadness of his shoulders and the heavyset muscles, I'm almost certain his torso will be chiseled to perfection.

The other is one of him and Ahren grinning at whoever is taking the photo, but the last one is of an older man. I can only guess it is Elian's dad because there's a slight resemblance with the dark hair and similar color eyes. His mouth, though, it's pursed in a severe line, as if he's angry at the world. Much like Elian is at times.

When Elian returns, he's holding a glass of white wine. "Something light, and you're only allowed one," he tells me in an authoritative tone, which makes me smile. I can't believe I'm here, in his house, having a drink with him. It feels slightly surreal.

"Thank you." I take a sip of the chilled liquid, and a burst of citrus flavors takes hold. It's delicious, and I tell him so. "This is a really good wine."

"And you're an expert, little deviant?" he

teases before tipping the tumbler he refilled and swallowing the honey-colored alcohol.

"Not an expert, but I know enough about the world of alcohol and drugs to last me a lifetime," I admit. Even though he's my teacher and I should probably not tell him all of this, I have a feeling my file already has the information I'm about to spew. "I've done bad things as a teenager, rebelled because of the world I grew up around, but I'm not … bad."

Elian regards me with a look that leaves me breathless. His shrewd, narrow gaze holds me in place, as if he's trying to gauge if I'm telling the truth or not. For a long while, we stare at each other in silence before he speaks.

"Tell me about the night you got plastered across the media," he says as he settles in one of the armchairs, resting his left ankle over his right knee.

"I don't—"

"I want to know what *your* version of the story is," he interrupts. So, he has read everything in my file.

"I was drunk, we were out partying, and things got messy. The night before, I was called into my father's office like I was one of his colleagues. He and my mother agreed that I would be sent away. A wayward teenager out of control. I was angry, and I did something stupid. It was a mistake I will not be repeating ever again."

Even though that's only part of the story I'm comfortable telling, Elian nods as if he's satisfied with my recollection. He sips his drink and continues staring at me.

"Now tell me the truth," he says suddenly. Leaning back in the chair, he grins when my mouth opens, then closes. "You can't lie to me, and you can't withhold information. If we're going to do this, you need to be honest. I have to know all those dark, little secrets you keep hidden behind those pretty, gray eyes."

"The past is just that," I tell him. "It's something I've walked away from. Surely that's something you can understand." A glint of frustration sparks in his stare, the blue reminding me of the ocean, deep and endless.

"Take off your dress," he orders suddenly, taking the topic of conversation away from my past and knocking it right into the present.

He glowers when I don't immediately obey. "I don't like repeating myself."

I set the glass down, never breaking eye contact with him. Slowly, torturously, I tug the hem up to my thighs. The higher it inches, the darker those cerulean orbs turn, and as the dress hitches past my hips, they're almost black. His pupils dilate, and I can hardly see the endless pools.

Once the dress is over my head, I drop it at my feet onto the soft, plush carpet. Elian's appraising gaze trails over me, from my hair, down my shoulders, over my breasts. And then slowly down my stomach, which has hummingbird wings fluttering wildly inside as he lowers his stare until he reaches my panties.

A rumble vibrates in his chest. He lifts his drink, taking a long swallow before lowering the glass and setting it on the table in front of him. When he rises to full height, he takes a step toward me, but he doesn't come close enough to touch.

Silently, he shoves his hands in his pockets before a small grin forms on his face. "On your knees," he finally speaks, the words booming around me even though he hasn't said it loudly. My nerves take hold as I slowly lower to my knees. This time, he gifts me a full, megawatt smile when he takes me in. "Are your panties getting wet, deviant?"

I nod, even though I know it's going to get me into trouble. Taunting the monster that lurks beneath those pretty, blue eyes is what I do best. Why change the habit now?

"I'm sure your clit is throbbing at the anticipation of what I'm going to do to you. Before I even touch that tight cunt, I'm going to see how good you are with your mouth." As he speaks, I watch as his hands move to the buttons of his shirt. Each one released from its confines. Once they're all loose, he shrugs off the material, allowing it to flutter to the floor.

His body is exquisite. Toned with dips and peaks that make my mouth water. He's not overly chiseled, but he doesn't need to be because every inch of him is pure muscle. This isn't a boy. This is a man.

He takes his time unlooping his belt from his slacks and then the zipper hisses, which only makes the tremble that's got a hold of my body worse. He's right—anticipation has most definitely got a hold of me.

"Open your mouth," he orders in a gruff, yet husky tone. "Stick out that pretty little tongue for me." The more he speaks, the more my need grows. I obey him without question, just like we agreed.

His slacks hang onto his hips. His hands dip into his boxer briefs, and he grips the thickness hiding inside, pulling it out until it's pointing right at me, angry and needy. The tip of him already weeping, wanting me.

I learned that men are least powerful when a woman is on her knees or on her back. Because we hold the power to say no. We can stop what we don't want if it's not acceptable. Elian closes the distance between us in two small steps and then his cock is touching my tongue. The saltiness of his arousal coating me, taunting me.

"Fuck," he growls when I wrap my lips around the head and gently suck. "Open your fucking mouth." I widen my hold on him. And he taps my tongue three times, as if he wants to slap me with the thick, angry shaft. He slides into my warmth, deep. When he hits the back of my throat, tears spring to my eyes, and he grins down at me.

Hello, Monster. Have you come out to play?

Elian's gaze darkens with desire. "Suck," is the only word that tumbles from his mouth and once more, like the good little deviant I am, I suck him. His cock throbs in my mouth, the thickness of it making me gag, but he doesn't relent. His hands fist my hair, holding me hostage. He is in control. Spit drips from my lips, down my chin and onto my chest. And from the look in his eyes, Elian loves it like that. And I have to be honest with myself—I'm wet, needy, and aching for more.

He pulls out slowly and thrusts back in, over and over again. I taunt and tease him with my tongue, sliding it along the shaft, and hum the moment he hits the back of my throat. The more he does it, the easier it becomes, and I focus past the gag reflex and take him even deeper.

His hands tighten in my hair, tugging until the bite of pain is merely a tingling sting. My clit, my pussy, my whole body is alight with need for him. I want to show him pleasure he's never felt before.

"Don't swallow just yet," he grits through clenched teeth, his eyes black and dangerous. His body seizes suddenly, and his cock throbs. His growl is feral and animalistic as he finds release, the salty arousal painting my tongue. When he pulls free, I'm sure a I'm mess. "You look beautiful with your makeup streaming down your cheeks," Elian says with satisfaction dripping from his voice.

My saliva has drenched the top of the bra I'm wearing, and my mouth has been marked by this powerful man. I open my mouth to show him his seed on my tongue. The motion has him smiling almost sadistically. I've given him pleasure, and I'm shaking with desire to do it again. The darkness inside him is awake and dancing under the moonlight. And I revel in the way he's looking at me.

"Good girl," he tells me. "Now swallow." And I do. The taste of him sliding down my throat. And I'm already hungry for more.

So much more.

ELIAN

I'm still lost in bliss when I see her swallow my release. The way she basks in how I used her is intoxicating. I want to do it again. Fuck, I want to do it over and over again until she's nothing but a trembling mess.

"Did you like me using your mouth like that?" I tip my head to the side, regarding her with amusement.

"Yes," she croaks, and I'm certain her throat is sore from the pounding. But the light that sparkles in her eyes tells me something else—she wants more too.

"Stand," I order gruffly, picking up my drink and swallowing the last mouthful. "You best finish your wine because I'm taking you to my bedroom. And when I take you home, you'll feel me all night and all day at school tomorrow."

Her eyes widen, but she obeys. Such a good little deviant for me. My cock is already hardening at the sight of her in the underwear I purchased. It's a perfect fit as well. I knew her body. I could tell from just looking at her the size, the shape, and I was right.

I watch Arabella drink down the wine before setting the glass on the table. With her delicate frame in front of me, I want nothing more than to show her what a monster I am. And I will.

"Go up the stairs, turn left, and walk all the way to the end of the hall. The bedroom in front of you will be where I want you to wait. On your knees, head bowed. And if you're not in the position I've requested when I get there, I'm going to punish you," I command, noticing a shiver wrack through her at my words, which only makes me grin.

Without a word, she turns and walks out of the living room, and I keep my gaze on her retreating form. The sway of her hips, the way her ass looks in those panties, and the slender legs that move with ease and grace makes the blood in my veins run hot.

Anticipation races through me, but I allow her time to get into the room, settle in position, and for me, time to calm myself. It's been a while since I've experienced such strong need, hunger to devour. Glancing at the window, I wonder if there are truly eyes on me like Ahren thinks. When my brother mentioned that he wouldn't be able to go away as I requested, I knew shit was going to hit the fan. One way or another, Arabella would find out about what I did.

But I can't allow that to shift my focus. I make my way up the stairs, one at a time, my lungs pulling in much-needed air as I reach the landing. Turning left, I fist my hands, knowing that soon I'll have her smooth flesh under my touch. I'll have her body beneath me.

Everything in life comes full circle.

When you find the moment where you're able to take what you have craved for so long, grab it. Don't allow it to disappear. The door beckons. I stop for a moment, calming the erratic heartbeat attacking my ribs.

When I twist the handle and step inside,

Arabella is on the floor, on her knees, waiting. This is most certainly not part of the plan, but being here with her seems to calm the rage of revenge that simmers in my veins. Like this, she isn't the daughter of the man who killed my father, and for a moment, I hope she doesn't ever find out the truth about her daddy.

"Look at me," I command as I lean against the wall, my arms crossed in front of my chest. Arabella lifts her gaze and locks it on mine. Her lips part, and I note how her tongue darts out, licking at the plump flesh. "Spread your legs. I want to see what I now own."

Watching her obey me makes my dick throb. I can't deny I'm enjoying this. Even if she doesn't realize who I am, I wonder just what her dad would say if he learned about his princess taking me inside her body tonight. He'd have a coronary if he knew his little girl was mine. I own her now.

"Touch yourself like you do in bed at night, thinking about me," I tell her, tacking on the last three words with a smirk gracing my mouth.

Those pretty steel orbs glaze over, desire burning in them as her hand slips between her slender thighs, and I watch how she shifts the material of the panties to the side to play with her cunt.

So. Fucking. Gorgeous.

She dips a finger inside, the wetness echoing toward me as she moves faster, picking up the pace as she finger-fucks her pretty pussy, but she keeps her gaze on me. Her mouth opens farther, a gasp of need spilling from her lips as she writhes on her fingers, and my cock aches.

"Stop." One word and her hand falls away, but I don't miss the whimper of frustration that follows her obedience.

I move toward her.

The moment my feet are at her knees, her head tips back, and she looks up at me. She looks so fragile, delicate on the floor of my bedroom. I lose myself in the scene before me. Her being mine, me not needing revenge, and just for a moment, I wonder if this could ever be more than a game.

"Stand."

She rises, a flower blossoming in front of me as I reach for the straps of her bra and tug at them, causing them to fall from her shoulders.

"Elian."

"Take off your panties," I order her, keeping my voice cool, yet my body is thrumming with need to devour every morsel of her beauty.

Her hands shift, pushing the scrap of material from her hips, and I allow my gaze to track the sensuality of how she moves, inching the panties to the floor. Once she steps out of them, I grip her shoulders and spin her around. Walking her over to the bed, I have her bend over the edge.

Her ass taunts me, her long legs tease me, and I spread them by pushing her feet wider. The view of her like this makes my cock weep. I'm so ready to sink into her. I discard my clothes without tearing my attention away from her because I can't. The need to see every part of her every second we're together burns through me.

I stalk to the nightstand. Finding what I need, I tear the foil wrapper and sheath myself as I take her in. She doesn't say anything again until I stop behind her, my hand gripping my shaft.

"Elian."

"If you want to stop, tell me now."

Arabella shakes her head, her hands fisting my sheets, her pure, pale skin a stark contrast to the dark blue material beneath her.

"No. I want you. Please just do it," she pleads, and I can't deny her request. I inch forward, feeling her warmth wrapping around me with every dip inside her. My hips drive forward without warning. Her breath whooshes from her as I fully seat myself inside her. Blackness overtakes my vision from the feel of her.

She's tight. So incredibly snug it's as if she were made to take me. I still all movement, allowing her to adjust to my size before I hear her whimper. I pull out and slam back in. Keeping my eyes shut, I focus on the way her walls pulse around me. The need to find release, for her and myself, overtakes the sick need for revenge that brought me to this moment.

I grip her hips, holding her steady as I pull out and drive back in, my body filling her, making every gasp and moan echo around us. The sound of skin slapping, of grunts and whimpers fill the air.

We move in sync as she pushes back

against me, as if she's trying to take me even deeper than I'm already fucking her. I lean over, reaching for her hair, wrapping the long, blonde locks around my fist, and I tug her toward me, her back arching beautifully as my lips find her earlobe.

"You're mine," I tell her, the honesty raw, scraping against my throat. I've felt pleasure in the past, but the way her cunt feels around my dick has me seeing fucking stars. My hips slam into her ass. The flesh in my hands will have bruises from my grip, but I don't give a shit.

I release her hip and trail my hand up her body, tweaking her nipple until I hear the scream I've been craving. A tear trickles from her cheek, and I can't stop the maniacal grin from forming on my lips.

My fingers wrap around her throat, the delicate column in my grasp, and I squeeze. Ever so lightly, but enough to make her pussy tighten around my shaft as I drive into her, all the way to the base.

Arabella mewls when I bite down on the fleshy earlobe, tugging it harshly between my teeth, along with my fingers stealing her breath and my cock balls-deep inside her. The gentle shaking of her legs against mine is the first sign of her impending release.

Keeping my hold on her throat, I release her hair and snake my hand between her thighs. The hardened nub under my taunting fingers is mine to play with. I circle her clit faster and faster as my hips piston against her.

"Oh god," Arabella cries out, her body tightening, her cunt sucking me harder, deeper, pulsing with her release, and I feel the wetness soaking me. I don't relent though. I send her into a second orgasm, and she screams as she shakes from pleasure wracking her body, her delicate frame trembling against me as I feel my own orgasm taking hold of me.

My spine tingles, euphoria skittering through me as I empty myself into the rubber, and I bask in the feel of her body accepting me, thickening and pulsing as I find bliss.

ARABELLA

I can't deny my morning is a mess of confusing thoughts. Last night was everything I wanted from him, but if I had to be honest, I do want more. My stomach somersaults when I recall what we did. My chest tightens when I think about how much pleasure Elian bestowed on me, but then after the salacious evening, Elian drove me home since I arrived at his in a taxi.

He made me happy. He'd claimed me without abandon. I never felt so completely and utterly owned, and I am already hungry for more. I recall the moment after we finally came down from the high of our orgasms.

"I think I better take you home," Elian's rough voice informs me as he helps me to my feet. My legs are still wobbly from what he's just done to my body. From the primal growl of him wanting me, claiming me, he seems almost as in shock as I am.

"Okay," is all I can force out as I watch him make his way to a walk-in closet. When he returns moments later, he's carrying a large tee and a pair of sweats that he hands to me. My dress is still on the floor downstairs, but I take the clothes.

"Put these on," he orders, but the tone of his voice is less commanding and more affectionate. Something I never expected from the man before me. There aren't any cuddles, and he doesn't hold me, but the heat in his gaze is enough to set my worried soul at ease.

Once we're dressed, we make our way to the front door and out to the garage where Elian opens the car door for me. Even as he weaves down toward home, my home, he doesn't speak. After he pulls up to the heavy, ornate gates, he turns to me and offers a smile.

"I don't usually spend the night with women," he informs me. Women. Is that how he sees me? "But I'll see you in class." I'm not sure if that's hope

253

in his voice, but my heart settles at the thought of him even wanting *to see me again.*

"Yes, you will," I respond, realizing it's a school day, which of course is why he'll see me. The stupidity of my thoughts causes me to blush, my cheeks hot, and I'm thankful it's dark.

But before I can get out of the car, Elian leans in and captures my lips with his. The softness of the kiss steals my breath. His fingers holding onto my chin, keeping me in place in order for him to lash his tongue along mine.

The contact causes my stomach to flip-flop wildly as he teases me until I'm trembling and needy for more heated kisses. When he pulls away, I almost whimper at the loss, and I'm sure he can tell how I'm feeling because there's a satisfied smirk on his lips.

"Go home. Be a good girl for me tonight," he informs me, and I know what he means. No touching.

"Goodnight," I respond before pushing open the car door. I can feel his eyes on me as I make my way up the drive, but by the time I reach the door, I know I've disappeared from his line of sight.

Now that the sun is sneaking up into the sky, the memories have a hold of me, and I'm nervous to see him at school. It's stupid because even though I know he wants me, there's still doubt that niggles at my thoughts, reminding me that I'm his student.

As I make my way to the gate, a cold shiver trickles down my spine, which has me spinning around. My gaze darts around the garden, toward the perimeter of the house, and back to the gate, which is slowly sliding open to let me out.

The feeling of someone watching me is visceral. It's as if they're right there, waiting for me to step out of the house. But that makes no sense. Black Mountain is a small town; it's safe. Nothing bad can happen here.

At least, that's what I tell myself. But instead of walking, I change my mind and go for the BMW aunt Midge said I could use if I wanted to. I would feel safer in a vehicle, and I'm not even sure why.

As I'm parking in the lot, I watch the other students head toward the building. Some are still chatting in groups on the lush green grass, and there are others who are on their own under the trees, lounging before class starts.

The eerie feeling I had moments ago is gone, but I can't shake the chill that's settled in my bones. I've had a stalker before, someone watching me, but he was caught, given a restraining order, and I know he won't come near me because he's more concerned with his name being kept out of the press.

A knock on my window has a scream tumbling from my lips, but when I glance up, I find Ahren grinning at me. "Boo," he says through the window, earning himself an eyeroll.

"What the hell are you doing?" I ask as I push open the door and exit the car.

"Hey, pretty girl," he greets me before pulling me into a hug. "I wanted to come and say hi," he tells me. When he steps back, I notice the glint in his dark eyes.

"What's that look for?"

When he shrugs, there's a smirk dancing on his lips, and I wonder if Elian said anything to him about what happened last night. If he did, I'm going to kill him.

"You spend more time here than you do at work," I tease as he grabs my backpack and falls into step beside me.

"I had to come see my brother," he says, his voice tense, but he doesn't show it in his expression when I glance his way. "Family shit I need to sort out before I head into work."

"How is work going?"

"Good. The apprenticeship is fun, something I've always wanted to do, and the fact that I'll possibly have something permanent once it's done is a bonus."

"That's amazing." We stop at the entrance to the school. Ahren has to head toward history, which is to my left, and I need to go right to English. "It feels like I haven't seen you in a while."

"A man like me keeps himself busy, pretty girl," he informs me with a wink. "Will you be at Elian's for dinner tonight?"

"I don't know."

"I'll pick you up. Clearly my brother is lacking in his wooing skills." He chuckles while shaking his head, his laugh infectious.

There's something about Ahren that sets me at ease. His personality is calming, and I enjoy being in his company. Not that Elian makes me uneasy, but he's more serious. "Let me know what time and I'll be ready," I tell him.

"It will definitely be nice to spend some more time with you," he whispers, keeping his voice low as other students pass by us. "And I think you should wear something breathtaking." His suggestion makes my stomach tumble wildly at the thought that this could be something more than just a friendly dinner.

"I'm sure I can muster up an outfit that will leave you both shocked." This time, I wink as I take my bag and wave goodbye to Ahren before heading to class. Even as I consider sitting down with Elian and asking him to tell me what's going on, what we are, after last night, I realize he was right. I do *feel* him.

"Hey, gorge!" Marleigh comes racing up behind me, slinging her arm around my neck as she joins me on the way to class.

"How are you?"

"Oh, you know …" Her words taper off, but the bright red on her cheeks tells me something has happened, and I'm actually excited to hear all the news about her and Alistor. The man she's been gushing over is someone I have yet to meet, but with the grin on her face, I'd say he's not doing all that bad.

"You do realize you cannot just leave it at that?" We're at the door to class, and as the rest of the students bustle in, I know we're not going to get to chat until after English.

"I'll catch you up on all the gossip once we're released from prison," Marleigh tells me, her gaze latching on the door behind me. But the grin on her face looks like she's about to burst with excitement at the details she's keeping.

"I need to know everything," I tell her as we laugh our way into the room and find our desks. I'm thankful for her friendship. At least with Marleigh, I can still enjoy my time in Black Mountain.

And of course, there is another reason that this small town has been a welcome distraction from the past, and his name is Elian Donati.

ELIAN

The class files in as the afternoon takes hold of the day, and I watch each student until I see her. The way her hair bounces in the ponytail, along with those slender legs, has my attention wrapped around her. Arabella doesn't look at me; instead, she smiles at her friend before they settle into their seats. Last night has been on my mind since I opened my eyes this morning, and I still can't believe she allowed me to take her so roughly. There's a slight bruise on her neck where my mouth had been only hours ago, and she hasn't hidden it.

"Good afternoon, class," I greet them as they fall silent, their eyes on the front of the room as they focus on me. The stack of papers in my hands will ensure a few groans echoing in the room shortly. "Today, we're having a pop quiz on the chapters we went over this week. I trust everyone is ready for this." I can't help grinning at the shuffling and unease that fills the classroom as they shift in their seats.

Moving toward the desks, I stop at each one, setting down the thick wad of pages that will soon be filled with scribbles and notes that are hopefully correct answers. When I reach Arabella's desk, I can't help but inhale deeply, taking in her perfumed scent.

The connection between us is evident when I set the pages down and her hand brushes along mine. Nothing about this is right. And if anyone were to look across at us, they would most definitely be able to tell from just the slight movement of her fingers along mine. It's more intimate than I care to admit.

The hunger I've felt for her since she first slammed into my chest has me wondering if my plans should be stifled. Revenge is a bittersweet emotion, and breaking her may just hurt me. I move on, the students shifting in their seats as they take in the first page of the quiz.

"You have an hour," I inform them as I make my way back to my desk. As I settle in to mark the previous class's quiz, I can't stop my attention from seeking her out, my gaze landing on her slender legs, and as she slowly opens her thighs, I have to cough to stifle a groan of pleasure at the sight before me.

She's seated herself in the front row, and from the soft pink material between her thighs, I can tell she's done it just to taunt me. Turning my attention to the papers on the desk, I settle in for the next sixty minutes, but every so often, my gaze rakes up, and I catch a glimpse of legs and pink.

By the time class is over, I'm hard as fucking stone. As they rise, heading toward my desk, I don't stand. Instead, I allow them to set their papers on the desk before exiting the room. But when Arabella reaches me, I glance up, locking my gaze on hers.

"I'd like to see you once everyone has left, please," I tell her, loudly ensuring the rest of the remaining students heard, including her best friend, Marleigh. The flash of annoyance on Arabella's face causes me to grin as I settle back in my chair, still hiding my thickened erection.

As soon as we're alone, I push to my feet and lean over the desk. Her pretty, stormy gaze flickers with uncertainty when my face comes close to hers.

"Close that fucking door," I bite out, gesturing with my chin toward the exit, which is now empty from the last body who's left my class. The click of the lock echoes loudly in the vast room.

Arabella returns to the desk where I'm perched on the edge, and I notice how her eyes land on the bulge in my slacks. Those lashes flutter, and I wonder if she's remembering what we did last night.

"Did you enjoy your little show?" I question, crossing my arms as I regard her with a narrowed gaze.

"I don't know what you're talking about," she sasses me, which doesn't help my frustration. Her hip juts out, and even though she's attempting to show her confidence, there's still a hint of uncertainty in her stance.

"Take your panties off."

Her mouth falls open, but she recovers

quickly. "What?"

"You heard me." I keep my expression schooled, but I want to smile. I want to laugh at the shyness so evident on those rosy cheeks.

Slowly, her hands inch under her skirt and then the scrap of material that covered her pussy falls at her feet. Arabella steps out of the item of clothing before picking it up and holding onto it. When I reach my hand out, her mouth drops into an O, but she doesn't argue. She knows better than to disobey. The small, cotton panties in my palm feels like a bomb about to go off.

I lift it to my nose, inhaling her scent, which only makes my dick jolt with need to sink into her. When I open my eyes, I crook my finger, calling her closer. She squares her shoulders, tipping her chin up as she walks toward me. My free hand reaches under the skirt, which I know she's shortened, and I cup her pretty cunt, my middle finger sinking into the wet heat I find at her center.

"This is your punishment for that display earlier," I tell her as I pump my finger in and out so slowly I earn a whimper of agonized pleasure from her plump lips.

"But … Elian," Arabella moans as my fingers taunt her, causing her hips to move against me as she takes her pleasure from my touch. With every second of her nearness, we're putting ourselves in danger. Anyone could knock on that door at any moment, but the wetness of her arousal dripping over my hand, the need painted on her pretty face, and every sound she makes forces me to continue.

I came here for one thing only—revenge.

But what I found was her. The broken girl with a pussy made for my cock. I put it down to lust. The hunger for connection, for a body against mine, but when her gaze locks on mine, her lips parting on a moan of pure euphoria, I wonder just how much more I can take without allowing myself to admit I have feelings for her.

Dipping two fingers inside, I feel her pulse. She's close, so I use my thumb to circle her clit, sending her spiraling over the edge. Her nails dig into my shoulders as she trembles in my arms.

"Fuck, Elian. You can't do that in here," Arabella admonishes me, and I can't help but chuckle. I retrieve my hand, bringing it up to my lips. The scent of her is intoxicating, and I slowly lick the arousal from each digit. The taste of Arabella is my high and my low—a reminder of what I'm enjoying even though it's against the rules.

"Trust me, little deviant, I'll do that and so much more while everyone fucking watches us. Do you think losing this job means much to me?"

"No. You don't need it, but that leaves the question from replaying in my mind." She tugs her skirt back into place while I devour the remnants of her from my fingers. "Why are you in Black Mountain?"

"The same reason you are," I tell her, but the lie burns my tongue as it slips from my mouth. There's a flicker of disbelief in her eyes, but she doesn't challenge me. "Tonight, you'll come to my house. We're having dinner."

"Ahren already invited me," she informs me coolly.

I'll need to talk to my brother. He didn't mention it to me when he popped in earlier to tell me about our little *problem*—the past coming back to bite us in the ass.

My gaze tracks Arabella as she makes her way to the exit. "Don't be late."

ARABELLA

When I get to Elian's house, I'm excited to spend a *normal* night with him and Ahren. Tonight offers up an opportunity to get to know the brothers without distraction.

I press the button of the doorbell. It doesn't take long for the door to whoosh open, and I'm met with the dark stare of Ahren Donati. The cocky smirk that curls his lips greets me as he pulls me into his arms and gives me a hug I wasn't expecting.

"Nice to see you, pretty girl," he says, his voice low, whispered, and I wonder if he doesn't want his brother hearing us.

"I hope you had a good day," I tell him as we break our hug and I follow him inside. The door shuts with a click behind us, and I follow Ahren through the entrance and into the back of the house. The kitchen is filled with the scent of delicious food, and my stomach growls, causing Ahren to chuckle.

"Hungry?"

"Yeah, I haven't eaten since breakfast," I tell him, reminding myself as to why I didn't get to have my lunch. And when I wanted to get something to eat after school, Elian kept me in his classroom sending me into euphoria with his fingers. The memory has me blushing.

"Not a good girl," Ahren murmurs in my ear, the heat of his breath fanning over my neck, causing goosebumps to rise on my skin. I chose a thin strapped dress, which hugs my frame, and under I have soft, satin panties, but no bra at all. I planned to tease Elian all night, and with Ahren here, it poses a challenge I'm sure I'm going to enjoy.

"I never once claimed to be a good girl," I sass the younger Donati and earn myself an amused chuckle.

"She's a very bad girl," comes the deep rumble of Elian Donati as he enters the kitchen dressed in a pair of black slacks and a matching button-up undone at the top, gifting me a view of his smooth skin.

"Oh?" This perks Ahren's attention, and I pray Elian doesn't tell him what I did in class today, but his smirk curls in challenge as he regards me.

"Indeed." He closes the distance between us, his hands landing on my hips, and my stomach does somersaults at the contact. *How can one man be so beautiful?* "She attempted being a little brat."

"I'm sure that should have earned her a spank," Ahren laughs as he pulls a bottle of beer from the fridge. At this response, I want the floor to open and swallow me whole as my cheeks heat with an embarrassing blush. He hasn't let go what I did in class today, but that only makes me tremble with anticipation of my upcoming punishment. Then Elian's mouth captures mine in a gentle kiss.

"She deserves so much more than that," he says, "which I'll sort out later. First we need to eat." He laces his fingers with mine, and in that moment, I feel as if I'm part of their family. The idea of being with him, with them, makes me feel special. "You look beautiful, by the way," Elian adds as we make our way through to the dining room, which has been set for three.

Elian sits right beside me with Ahren across from me. The air has shifted; something is about to happen, and I'm not entirely sure of what it is. We're served dinner by the lady who had ushered me into the house on my first visit.

Before she leaves us, she tells Elian everything for dessert has been set out. Then we're alone.

"Take off your dress. Leave it on the floor beside you," comes the voice from my left, sending cold awareness through me. My gaze snaps to his, finding no amusement shining in it. "I don't like repeating myself, deviant," he practically growls. And the dinner I thought would be endearing and an opportunity for me to learn more about the brothers, Elian flips on its head. For a beat, neither Ahren nor I move. We don't reach for our cutlery. Even though I'm starving, I wait.

My glance falls on Ahren who's smirking with utter satisfaction on his face. He watches me for a moment before saying, "You must have really pissed big brother off today."

"Don't be ridiculous." The words tumble from my lips when I look back at Elian who doesn't look at all like he's joking. "You're serious?"

"Oh, I'm deadly fucking serious," he answers in a husky growl.

Fine. He wants me to show off for his brother. This is his funeral.

I slip the straps over my shoulders, but before I can allow the material to fall, Elian's hand grips my wrist, and he presses it against my breasts. There's no hint of a bra, and his glare burns right through me. From the corner of my eye, I notice Ahren shaking his head, his smirk still firmly in place as he picks up his cutlery.

"I didn't say we could eat yet," Elian's voice cuts through the air, and Ahren glances up to arch a brow at his brother. My dress, still firmly in place, covers me, but the way Elian is watching me, I may as well be naked. "This naughty girl …" Elian traces a slow, white-hot path over my shoulder with his fingertip, tugging the straps back up, leaving goosebumps to explode over my skin. "She was in my classroom, showing off her wet panties." In an attempt to taunt me, he circles my nipple over the material gently before moving onto the other. They're hardened peaks, and I know Elian's rock hard because he shifts on his seat.

When he leans in close, his warm breath fans over my neck, causing me to shiver. His touch trails lower. My stomach tumbles wildly as I watch Ahren sit back, enjoying the show. The way his gaze burns me tells me our friendship is so much more.

"Now, you're going to eat your dinner like a good girl and then I'm going to show you just what naughty teases get when they misbehave." The illicit promise that skitters over my skin in a hushed whisper makes me squirm in my seat.

Elian sits back, picking up his cutlery, and both men settle into their meal, leaving me needy and frustrated. My appetite is raging, but it's definitely not for the food in front of me. But I behave and pick up the knife and fork before digging into the delicious dinner.

The risotto is probably the best I've ever tasted, and the grilled vegetables along with the beef have me moaning as the flavors of rosemary has my tastebuds tingling. Everything seems to melt on my tongue, and I can't help but groan in pleasure.

"If you keep that up, I'll have to put you on the table and devour you. I'm sure Ahren won't mind," Elian warns under his breath, but it's loud enough for his brother to hear.

"I'd like to know more about our pretty girl. Remind me again where you're from. Miami, am I right?" Ahren asks suddenly, causing both Elian and I to snap our gazes toward him.

"Yes, born and raised," I tell him, feeling Elian stiffen beside me. His hand on my thigh tightens, as if he's warning me of something, but I'm not sure what.

"Mm …" Ahren's dark stare flicks to his brother. Silent questions dance in his eyes as they regard each other. It's strange—the interaction is almost as if they're reading each other's minds.

"What?" I find myself asking, glancing between the men, but neither of them says anything. "If you won't tell me, I'll leave." I push the chair back, causing a loud screech along the tiles before I turn for the exit.

I don't make it out of the dining room when hands snake around my waist, lifting me against a hard body I know is Elian. He spins on his heel, causing me to face Ahren who's seated, watching the display.

Elian stalks to the table where he puts me down and grips my shoulders. I'm leaning back against the smooth wooden surface, and Elian is looming over me, causing me to want to scoot back.

His hands are on me in the next second, one gripping my neck, holding me in place, while the other snakes down between my thighs, and he finds what he's looking for. My panties, which are wet.

"Did you like showing off to me like that?" he questions as embarrassment takes hold of me. I can't answer though because his confident fingers explore my center, and I'm hyperaware that his brother is inches from me.

"Fuck you, Elian Donati," I bite out. He grins at me as he hovers over me. Ahren can't see anything, but embarrassment still heats my cheeks.

"Did you want to show Ahren what's mine?" His voice is low, gravelly as it vibrates through his chest. Tears spring to my eyes as his hand taunts me. Dipping inside me, he finger-fucks me on the table while the dark stare to my left watches.

"No." My voice is croaky, but I finally voice my response to him. "I don't."

"Good," he growls, the words vibrating over my lips as he leans in. "Get the fuck out, brother. I have to sort something out." His order is clear, but he doesn't relent. He continues opening me, his hand moving so fast I can hear my wetness. which only has my cheeks burning hotter, and I'm sure I'm bright red.

Ahren moves. I see his face passing from the dining room and out toward where the living room is, but his stare was hot on me. A blush creeps down my neck, down to my chest, and it takes hold of every inch of me as Elian crooks his fingers, pressing that spot inside me that has me screaming as my release hits me.

My thighs shake, my body trembles, and my toes curl as I attempt to claw the table to find purchase, and all thoughts of embarrassment and shyness fade into black as sparks dance across my eyelids.

And for a moment, I'm lost in bliss.

HIM

THE PRESENT

Filth.

Disgusting filth.

Rage boils through me as the memory of her takes hold. She ran away, but I was always here, following, watching, waiting. I have had to bide my time, but what she doesn't realize is that her precious lover is nothing but a liar. Perhaps that's why they're so good together. They're both cut from the same cloth.

I move through her bedroom, opening the drawer where I find lacy panties I'm sure she wears for him. Picking up one pair, I bring it to my nose, knowing it won't have her scent on it, but I can only imagine. The memory of that night burns brightly.

If only she'd remember. If only she'd shut her eyes and see my face. I know she feels me watching. My cock hardens as I pull it from my sweatpants. Wrapping the lace around the shaft, I stroke myself, remembering her being taken in his bedroom. I wonder if she's ever fucked him on his desk in the classroom. It's the only place I can't see her.

My hand moves faster, the delicate material sending waves of pleasure through my body. Grinning as I feel my release nearing, I jerk my dick until my release coats the material, and euphoria of tarnishing her perfectly made up lie overwhelms me. Jet after jet spurts all over her underwear, and I can't help but grin as I empty myself over the panties she'll have against her pretty whore cunt.

Wiping myself clean, I set the messed underwear into the drawer, and I shut it before righting myself. She'll come home, and I know she won't look in there until morning. And when she does, I hope she's as disgusted by it as I am by her.

Soon, little girl. So, fucking soon.

ELIAN

I sit down on the sofa while Arabella joins me. Ahren's seated across from us on the armchair, a drink in hand as he smirks over at me. But there are still questions in his eyes. He knows she's also from Miami, where we're from. And I know I'll have to answer to him soon, but not right now.

Now I can focus on my girl. Arabella enjoys being degraded, but I haven't even taken her that step further. With Ahren, I know she's safe. She doesn't need anything more because that fucking orgasm she had on the dinner table nearly took me over the edge with her. I have a feeling my brother wasn't happy to leave us alone.

The last time we were together with a woman in the same room, it was *her*, and that was a fucking mistake. I helped my little deviant to her feet, righting her dress and sitting her on the chair, and I could still feel her tremble.

I drape my arm across the back of the sofa, my one hand on her shoulder, and I lean in before pressing a gentle kiss to her cheek. "Next time you want to taunt me, remember this night and what I did to you," I warn her. "Because if you try to top me from the bottom, I will do worse to return the favor." My voice is drenched in a promise, and even though I'm sure she won't take a chance again, my cock is hard at the possibility of fucking her in front of her whole goddamned class.

"You're ridiculous," she tells me, but all I do is chuckle in response.

"You both should go out to the cabin," Ahren says suddenly. "It will be nice out there this weekend." I consider this for a moment, and I'm tempted to refuse him. I wouldn't mind heading out of town, taking Arabella to the middle of nowhere so I can make her scream my name even more.

"Cabin?" Her eyes widen as she looks over at me, and I realize my brother just threw me under the fucking bus. She looks excited, and I realize I'm going to have to take her.

"Yeah, our family has a cabin out in the woods, beautiful with a waterfall." He lays it on thick. *Asshole.* Ignoring my glare, he continues. "You could leave Saturday morning. Come back on Sunday night. Ask your aunt and see if she'll allow it."

"I'm sure she won't mind. But I would like that." Arabella's voice is filled with excitement, and even though I'm tempted to squash it, I know I can't because I want her to be happy. Which is ridiculous because I wanted her to pay for her father's sins. But, once again, I wonder if he is still alive, and if he is, that may be a hinderance to what I'm developing with her.

"Sure." Even though I'm not sure she even knows where he is, I can use her to lure him out. "I'll drive us up there this weekend." And as the night wears on, my mind continues playing out scenarios of just how I can finally get my revenge.

My brother is fucking ridiculous with his bright ideas. Taking her on a romantic weekend getaway isn't going to change the fact that we're just fucking. Forbidden with benefits. But when he brought it up at dinner a few days ago, Arabella seemed so excited to get out of town, and we haven't had time alone together. Maybe I can finally confess my reasons for being here, for knowing her. But if I did tell her the truth, there's no doubt she'd hate me.

And why would I have a problem with that? I don't fucking know.

Each day that passes, she's burrowing herself into my life, into my mind. And even though I know I can't fall for her, something's happening. The need to protect her has overtaken me, and I want to lock her in my bedroom and keep her there.

My phone buzzes as I make my way to the garage and I notice my call ahead to have the cabin stocked with food and drinks has been completed. I haven't had time to go up there in a while, and I know the place had been empty for a couple of months.

At the car, I shove my bags into the trunk

and shut it before heading to the driver's door. Once I'm seated, I start the engine and head down the drive to the gate. My plan is to take Arabella to the cabin. It's our family's private residence, and we'll have some quiet time to get to know each other.

The night she got arrested seems to be a block for her, but more than that, I have a feeling she may know where her dad is. If she does, I'll hopefully be able to coax it out of her while gifting her with endless orgasms. All I need to do is remind myself she's nothing more than a pawn in this game.

When I pull up to the house, Arabella is standing at the gate, her face a picture of worry as I come to a stop and she races toward the car. She shoves the small suitcase into the trunk before pulling open the passenger side door. The moment she's beside me, her breath whooshes from her lips.

"What the hell is wrong?" I stare at her, taking in the anxiety etched all over her pretty face. I can't deny she's beautiful. It's not something I should be noticing, but I'd have to be blind not to see it.

"Nothing," Arabella breathes before she offers me a smile. But it doesn't meet her eyes, and I know something is wrong.

"I don't like lies, little deviant," I grit out, my fingers squeezing the fucking steering wheel so hard my knuckles turn white.

"I just … it feels like someone is watching me," she finally admits, and I can't deny my blood burns hot. "And …" Her words taper off when she twists her hands in her lap, sending my rage through the fucking roof.

"And fucking what, Arabella?"

"The other night, after dinner," she starts, lifting those stormy eyes to mine. "Well, the next morning, I found … I mean …" I'm about to grab her and shake the information from her, but then she whispers, "I found a mess in my underwear drawer."

All I see is red. My rage is at boiling point. "What?"

"It's as if someone … It was all dried, but it wasn't something I'd dropped in there."

Starting the engine, I pull out onto the road, the tires squealing against the tar, and we shoot forward, zero to fucking sixty in a milli-fucking-second.

"Elian," Arabella tries to call to me, but I'm too enraged to think straight. My focus on the road ahead blurs, and I know I should pull over, but I don't. Instead, I race for the highway which will take us out of Black Mountain and up toward the cabin. She doesn't try again. She doesn't touch me. We just sit in silence as I simmer at what she just said.

We're nearing the cabin when I finally speak, attempting to keep my voice calm. "Why didn't you tell me the day it happened?"

"I was scared. I don't know." She lifts her watery gaze to mine. "I think I know who it is, and … I'm not sure he's going to stop." Her admission makes every part of me go rigid.

I kill the engine when we get to the cabin and turn toward her. "I want all the details. His name, age, where he lives, anything you know about him. Am I understood?" I'll sort the bastard out. He'll never come near her again.

I push open the door and exit the vehicle, making my way toward her side. Offering her my hand, she accepts with a small smile, and I know I need to distract her from what happened.

This is a good thing. But the problem is, it's all my fucking fault she's in this mess.

Inside the cabin, I watch as Arabella moves through the comfortable living room, which is furnished with soft couches and bean bags. We used to party out here, but since I started teaching, my focus had shifted from parties to revenge.

The girl before me spins on her heels, meeting my stare. "This is perfect," she tells me with a grin on her face. The haunted look she had in the car has dissipated, but I'm certain it will return.

Unless I do something.

ARABELLA

He has a smirk across his lips, but there's emotion shining in his eyes I can't quite put my finger on. It could be guilt, or worry, I'm not sure.

"It's one of my favorite places." Elian moves toward me, stopping inches from me. "We're alone here." His words skitter over my skin, making me shiver. "And nobody can hear you scream my name."

"Is that a promise?" I tease, twining my arms around his neck, and I hold on as he lifts me against him. My legs wrap around his waist, but he doesn't walk us into the bedroom. Instead, he settles on the couch, leaving me straddling him.

"Tell me your secrets, little deviant," he says, not entirely a question, but also not an order. "I want to know you. Tell me about your folks, about you growing up."

He seems genuinely curious. I open my mouth to respond, but I'm not sure how. The reminder of why I came to Black Mountain flicks through my mind, bringing with it the heartache I've shoved down into the recesses of my soul.

"If I talk about it, I'll only break down."

"Let me see you," Elian pleads. Cupping my face in both hands, he pulls me toward him, bringing our mouths within inches of each other. "I want to see you bared for me."

"I can only do it physically."

"That doesn't work for me, little deviant," he says confident. "I want it all. Every dark part of you." His hands release my face, and one moves to my neck, the other trails down and grips one of my breasts. Elian squeezes harshly, stealing my breath along with sending pleasure skittering through me. "Give me everything." He practically growls the command, and I feel it. Something deep inside me breaks loose from the box I'd put it in, and tears spring to my eyes. "Did Daddy hurt you, sweetheart?" Elian coos. "Did he make you cry?" Another question as his one hand releases my breast and grips my hip, moving me over his hardening cock.

Tears trickle from my eyes when I think about the funeral. The words my mother muttered were nothing more than fabricated emotion. Just like the woman herself. She didn't want me. She never loved Dad. All she wanted was the fame that came with being a politician's wife.

"Tell me, deviant," Elian says. "I want it all."

"My father died. He was killed, and I never got to say goodbye," I finally spit out as anger overtakes the pain, but Elian's hands don't relent. His grip on my neck is still harsh, along with the way his hand moves me over his crotch. "And I was taught not to feel."

"Feel this," he says, lifting his hips to press against my core. "That's real. Not some fucking rule about not feeling emotion."

"My mother didn't like my tears. She never enjoyed seeing my pain or listening to my heartbreak." I don't know why, but the admission falls from my lips. His fingers grip my hips, his rough fingertips sending shivers through me as he holds me like I'm a fragile doll. His possessive hold cutting the safety net that I'd so perfectly laid my pain under.

"She's a fucking liar," Elian sneers as if he knows her personally. "Emotion is what makes us feel alive. The happiness and the sadness," he continues as he taunts me with pleasure and steals my breath.

"How do you know?" I whisper, and we both still. Our gazes locked. My mouth still inches from his. "How can living with heartbreak make you feel alive? I just want to be numb. This here," I say as I roll my hips, giving me the friction, I crave. "That's the only thing that ever made sense to me. The night I was arrested, most people think it's because I was partying it up ..."

"Close your eyes," he orders, and I do. I obey him like I've done so many times before. "Tell me what happened that night." He pulls me against him, my head resting on his shoulder, and I can smell the spicy scent of his cologne.

"I ... I ... I broke into his house." The truth

tumbles free from my lips.

"Whose house?"

Sighing, I realize I have to tell him. Tears fall from my lashes, wetting my face, but I don't swipe them away. I'm once again obeying Elian and allowing the pain to take hold of me. "When I was sixteen, there was a boy I crushed on. He was the quarterback of our school team. Perfect in every way, but I learned that night, perfection didn't exist."

Elian goes rigid under me, and I picture his face painted with rage. I'm not sure why, but it pushes me to continue with my story. The same story I'd locked up tight along with my father's death.

"We went back to his place after the game. I thought I'd be the special girl he took to prom. I wanted to be his high school sweetheart." A humorless laugh tumbles from my lips. "But he was convinced with a couple of glasses of wine I'd be up for anything."

"Arabella ..."

"I wasn't like that. Not then anyway. He broke me, tore me open, and I was never the same. I couldn't tell anyone because my mother would've blamed me, and my dad, he would've killed the boy. I couldn't have my dad going to jail. I loved him."

"So, you stayed silent," Elian whispers, and I nod against his shoulder. "And the bastard is the one you feel is now stalking you?" Another nod, and more tears fall. Elian's arms wrap around me gently, pulling me closer as he stops all movement. He doesn't say anything more. We sit in silence as the day turns to night, but his warmth calms me after a long while. I haven't broken down like this before, but having him near me, holding me safely, I allow myself to break.

When he finally stands, lifting me along with him, he takes me to the kitchen where he sets me on a stool and heads to the fridge. Elian opens two beers, setting one down for me, and he swigs the other. Silently, we move through the kitchen making dinner. As we sit and eat, Elian seems distracted, angry. Just before eleven, he walks back into the living room from the bathroom dressed in a pair of sweatpants.

"Come here, sweetheart," he says with his hand reached out to me. When I close the distance, he takes me, and we walk into the bedroom.

I'm nervous. I never once expected to admit the truth of that night to him, but here I am. Elian turns to me, a small, almost sad smile curves his lips.

"Take all your clothes off and lie back on the bed."

I do as he says. When I'm comfortable, he takes me in like he did the first time we had sex. And then, he moves onto the mattress, kneeling at the foot end as he takes each of my legs, planting gentle kisses on my ankles, trickling them up to my inner thighs.

He mimics his actions on both sides before he reaches my pussy, and his mouth turns me into a trembling mess. His tongue darts inside me while his fingers taunt my entrance. He holds my pussy open for his tongue and teeth to lick and bite at me.

Slowly, he dips two fingers into me, and I almost shoot off the bed when his teeth latch onto the bundle of nerves at my center. His talented kisses send me screaming over the edge. Fragments of bliss spark through me as I scream out his name.

With the agility of a predator, he slides over me, pressing a kiss to my lips, and I taste myself on his tongue when he slides it along mine. His movements are not at all what I'm expecting, it's … romantic.

Something shifted when he slid inside me seconds ago. It wasn't rough or angry. There was a gentleness to his kisses and the way his body took mine. I'm lost in the way his hands hold me, in the way his lips steal mine, swallowing every moan and whimper.

As my lashes flutter closed, I attempt to hold back the tears as realization hits me in the chest. I care about him. It can't be love. Not just yet, but the way he seems to be claiming me tells me that he feels this connection as well.

He is everything I never knew I wanted.

This is everything I never knew I needed.

And I realize in that moment, this would be everything that would haunt me until I admit the truth to him. But in doing so, I might lose him. His body moves over me, his hips slapping against mine as I take him deep. He thickens, stretching my walls, and I welcome the bite of pained pleasure that shoots down my spine.

I dig my nails into his back, holding on, craving more. His mouth captures my nipple, biting down harshly, which sends pain zinging from the hardened bud down to my clit. My toes curl when he mimics the action on the other breast.

Arching my back, I press my body closer to his, needing to be against him. To feel every hard valley and every dip of his muscles as he works my body into a frenzy of euphoria. I can't look at him, but I feel his gaze burning me, boring a hole right to my soul.

Even in this pleasurable moment of bliss, I know I have to tell him why I was arrested.

"Come for me," he pleads, his one hand circling my clit as he thrusts into me, harder, faster, and I cry out when he pinches the bundle of nerves lighting my veins on fire with pure, unraveling hedonism.

In the dark, we're safe with our dirty little secret, but the harsh light of day would forever scorch us for our actions. The room is bathed in shadows, but when I open my eyes tomorrow morning, I know there will be harsh sunlight spilling the truth to the man who's now cocooned against me.

I hid my pain for so long that as Elian's arm wraps around me possessively, I find the tears I'd been holding back slowly trickle down my face. Every person I've ever loved has left me. And I know that Elian will also disappear. I force the images of him walking out from my mind, but there's only so much I can fight because I know I can never fully expunge him from me.

"This could never be more." His nighttime admission snaps me from my thoughts, but even as he says the words, his hands never strayed, his arm never left me. "You know we shouldn't have done this."

I nod to the darkness. "I know. I realized it the moment you kissed me."

"And you didn't stop me?" His question isn't meant to hurt. It's genuinely curious.

I smile. There's no way I could ever have stopped him. Even if I wanted to. My heart is slowly splintering when I realize what he's saying. But I whisper, "How could I?"

He flips onto his back, pulling me astride his hips, my body looming over his. His guilt-ridden stare bores into mine, searching, making me blink because I'm afraid of what he'll find there.

His rough hands give my ass one last hard squeeze before he leans up, resting his weight on his elbows. I'm still straddling his waist, not wanting to break the connection of his cock against my pussy.

Heat sizzles through the air, warming my skin, and I can't help touching his smooth, tanned skin one more time. As if I'm memorizing every line, each sip of his abs and peak of his muscles.

Perfect.

Only, he isn't.

He looks at me for a long time, as if he's trying to tell me something but not wanting to admit the truth. His gaze holds secrets, just like I've kept mine safe. His mouth opens, then shuts. And it's as if he makes his decision.

"I can't do this without hurting you. It has to end." He finally utters the words I'd been dreading to hear. Cold seeps through my veins, understanding that he's not mine. The lump in my throat threatens me, growing thicker with every second. My eyes burn, the watery emotion about to spill, but I blink it back and nod.

"Yes." My voice is scratchy, and I admonish myself for the lump in my throat.

Stupid girl.

ELIAN

I left Arabella at home. Her house is the safest place for her to be tonight. I'm not sure if she felt the pain that I had experienced when I made love to her last night, but I have a feeling she did. Her intelligent mind may be playing out a variety of scenarios right now, but the one that's the truth will never even pass her mind.

All the lies that we were built on had come to a head, and it's my fault she was in danger. That's not something I can live with. Guilt ate away at me. I needed to ensure her safety. I started out thinking she would be nothing more than a passing phase, but it turns out, Arabella Davenport has burrowed herself into my fucking soul.

I never realized I even had one until she looked into my eyes last night and told me what she'd been hiding. I knew about the boy, but the truth that spilled from her lips has my blood burning hot in my veins. The thought of anyone forcing themselves on a woman is not something I abide by. Which is the reason I'm out here in the dead of night.

The rage that passes through me as I pull into the lot of the old abandoned warehouse is nothing compared to the violence I'm about to inflict. Shrugging on my jacket, I make my way to the door which is slightly ajar. When I sent that message earlier, I had made the decision. This is what I was born to do. My father would be proud of my dealing with bullshit. A rogue bastard needs to be dealt with.

My footsteps crunch on the cold, wet concrete. The floor has been ripped up in places, which breaks as I head deeper into the chilly expanse. Waiting for me is the asshole I'm about to rip to shreds. He's watching me as I near him.

"What the fuck do you think you're playing at?"

He doesn't respond right away. Instead,

someone walks out into the dim light, and her gaze locks on mine. "Mr. Donati," she greets with a sly smile that makes my stomach coil. I didn't think I'd come face-to-face with her, but here she is.

"You came a long way just to see me," I remark, meeting the same stormy eyes I've been looking into for the past month. The only difference is that the woman standing before me is much older and much more sinister than her daughter.

"When I last spoke to you, I was under the impression you were going to do as I asked," she tells me, which only makes me laugh.

"Do you really think I'm going to obey you when your fucking husband killed my father?" I bite out, my teeth grinding against each other, causing my jaw to tick with frustration. "I don't bow down to anyone. I'm a Donati. And your little boytoy over here has gone too far."

"I'll decide what's too far," Pandora Davenport tells me with a smirk creasing her lips. No wonder her husband was happier disappearing than spending time around her. The bitch is a psychopath.

"Actually," I respond, pulling the gun from my pocket. Cocking it, I lift it slowly, aiming it at the bastard's face. "I'll decide where we go from here."

"Have you fallen in love with her?" The sheer shock that's painted across Pandora's features is clear as it drips from her question. *Have I?* No. I can't love her. She's just a girl I enjoyed fucking.

"I don't deal well with men who do bad things."

"Does she know who you truly are?" Her challenge has me gripping the gun harder, my fingers wrapping around the handle, my finger hovering over the trigger. "Because I think if my dear little girl found out about the man she's spreading her legs for, she'll run in the opposite direction."

"That's better than someone raping her when she's underage?" I sneer, my gaze locked on the piece of scum whose expression tells me he didn't realize I knew the truth.

"That's just a story she's made up to get attention."

"Is it?" This time, my glare lands on the

older woman. "Why don't we ask him?" My focus zeroes in on the man I'm about to kill. "Tell me."

"Hey man, she was up for anything when she walked into my bedroom. You would know. The little bitch opens her pretty pussy for any dick offering." He chuckles, his words dripping through me like poison, and my finger slips, sending a bullet flying, hitting him right in the shoulder. *"What the fuck man?"*

"Tell me the fucking truth." My command bounces off the metal walls that surround us. "I don't like repeating myself." Another bullet hits him in the knee, and I aim the next for his crotch, which has the asshole howling in agony.

"Okay! Okay!" His hands hold onto his dick, which is gushing blood. "I did … I mean, she was …" I cock the gun once more before he finally admits, "Wait! Okay, I did. Yeah, I forced her. I didn't think it was an issue."

That's all I needed to hear, and the last bullet hits him right in the chest, just missing his heart. Stalking toward his shuddering form, I straddle his body before gripping his neck with one hand, and squeezing, watching his eyes bulge from their sockets.

"You're filth. Rot in hell."

"Quite the dramatics," Pandora says when I finally rise to meet her stare. The stench of metal fills my nostrils, but I've never felt more alive. Taking someone's life is intoxicating.

"Where is your husband?"

"I don't know. He flew to Europe to hide out, but my men lost him. We haven't been able to track him again." The woman came to me when she found out about her dear husband's illegal activities within the political sphere. He had bought votes, paid off informants to learn more about his competition, and not long after being elected by a landslide, he had been caught with a prostitute, which sent Pandora over the edge.

She found out about his underhanded business with my father and three months ago, she came to me and asked for my help by appealing to my need for revenge. Pandora poked the proverbial sleeping bear and here I am.

Pandora realized her husband had hired guns to come after my dad, and that's when she realized I would help put an end to her husband. But then I made the deal when I saw the one thing her husband would never leave behind. I wanted something for my trouble. I didn't need money, so I asked for the one thing I knew she couldn't refuse me—Arabella.

"Go to her. Tell her everything, but mark my words, she'll never believe you. Her father will never come for her."

Her words cause my chest to tighten with anxiety. I don't know why. I never truly wanted to hurt Arabella. Pandora has just confirmed her husband is alive. Now, I want him to come out of hiding. But even as I think it, I know it's a lie because I ended up falling for the beauty who was merely a pawn in my game.

"I don't necessarily need her to believe me," I inform the woman before me. "I just need her to have a life free from the darkness." My admission has her dark brow arching.

"You'd be surprised what my daughter is capable of. Personally, I think you'd make a good couple. She's a deviant, and you, Mr. Donati, are now a cold-blooded killer. Surely, you can see it's a match made in heaven."

Shaking my head, I shrug at her words, but I do believe them because Arabella was made for me. I turn to leave before I call over my shoulder, "When that man you married returns, he'll pay for his sins. When I find him, your daughter will be an orphan."

She doesn't run even though she knows what's coming. She just waits for it, and when I pull the trigger, I hear the slump of her body.

"She will never forgive you," Pandora speaks with finality before I walk out, leaving both bodies for cleanup. You can take the man out of the organization, but you can never cleanse the violence from his blood.

ARABELLA

I haven't seen Elian since he dropped me off at home. He didn't even explain what was happening. All he told me was to stay indoors. Our *goodbye* wasn't confirmed, and even though he hasn't contacted me today, I'm nervous about what's coming. It's as if a storm is about to hit, and I'm caught in the center of it.

"Hi." A girl grins at me with a wide smile and perfect teeth. She's dressed in the academy's uniform, but I've never seen her before. Granted, the place is massive, so she most probably is a student and I've just never met her.

I don't want to be rude, so I greet, "Hi."

"You're Arabella, right?" she says. Lowering her voice, she continues before I can respond.

"I'm Evette," she informs me, although I'm still unsure as to why she's introducing herself.

"Nice to meet you. Is there something you wanted?" I shrug my blazer off and throw it along with my backpack into the car before shutting the door.

She's close, like really close to me because I can feel her beside me. "I have a note from your dad," she tells me, causing my stomach to drop to my feet like a lead weight.

Spinning around, I stare at her in confusion. "What?"

Instead of responding, she hands me an envelope. It's not big, but it's thick, as if something has been folded a few times before being shoved into it. Sealed shut, I can't even glimpse what's inside to make sure she's not bullshitting me.

"Are you playing some fucked-up game?"

"Arabella," my name is called before the strange girl can say anything more, and I turn to find Elian stalking up to us, urgency painted across his expression. His gaze lands on the girl. A hint of something flashes in his eyes— recognition perhaps—before he turns toward me. "Are you okay?" he asks me, and I realize I must still have shock painted across my expression.

"Yeah. I guess." My response to Elian is whispered, and I glance over to ask the girl who she is or why she had this, but she's already disappeared into the crowd of students. "That was fucking strange."

"What?" Elian questions. I wish he could just wrap me in his arms right now, but we can't do that since we're on school property. And even though he's standing at my car right now, it doesn't look as if anything is going on because he's kept his distance.

"She said she had a message from my father and then handed me this," I tell him, glancing at the envelope in my hands once more. There isn't anything written on the front nor the back, which begs the question—*was she just some psycho from back home?*

"If you want me to get rid of—"

"No, it's okay," I interrupt him, needing some space to clear my head. I shouldn't even be near him. After the cabin, we didn't say anything more. Even though the weekend was romantic, I knew it was his way of putting distance between us. "I'll talk to you later." I don't look at him again before sliding into the driver's seat and starting the engine. But as I'm pulling out of the lot, I notice Elian's rage-filled expression as I leave him behind.

I'm not sure how I manage to get home. Even though the drive is short, I'm not focused on anything other than the girl and the envelope. After I've parked, I'm out of the car, heading into the house with my belongings, and make a beeline for my bedroom.

Things in Black Mountain have been amazing. I've had time to focus on school, and I've also become attached to Elian. I shouldn't have, but each day I'm with him I feel myself falling. My emotions are all over the place when I finally sit on my bed and rip open the envelope before pulling out the thick letter.

Unfolding it, I take in the familiar handwriting, and my heart stutters. A lump forms in my throat when I read the first two words, "Dear Princess," and my eyes prickle with tears. Setting the letter down, I attempt to breathe through the pain lancing my chest.

It's been almost four months, yet it feels like yesterday when my mother told me dad was gone. That he died.

The moment replays in my mind, over and over again. So real. It was so real, I never questioned it. I didn't ask why we couldn't have an open casket. I just accepted what she told me as the truth.

As much as she's been aloof with me most of my life, I didn't think she would lie to me, not about something like this. It makes no sense for her to have fabricated a story like this to hurt me.

I pick up the letter again as confusion settles in my gut. With a watery gaze, I settle against the headboard and prepare myself for an onslaught of emotions I'm certain will rip me apart.

Dear Princess,

All my life, I've tried to make sure you're safe. I failed because if you're reading this, I'm gone. Not dead, but I should be. None of this will make sense to you but know that I'm always watching from afar. I never once wanted you to get in the middle of my mistakes, and I always kept you from finding out the truth about me. I wanted nothing more than to be your hero, but instead, I was the villain in this particular story.

It's time you find out who I am, and I wanted to be the one to tell you. The job got to me. After years of playing by the rules, I ended up breaking them, and it took me down a dark path, which forced me to do things I'm ashamed of, and I never wanted you to see me in that light.

I took a life.

I stole from a family who will happily see me dead before they forgive me. When I made the choice to do it, I never thought of the repercussions, and that was my mistake. I should've focused on my family instead of wanting my seat in the White House. Promises were made, and vows were broken.

I got into bed with a dangerous man, and I ended up putting our lives in danger. But, in saying that, I now realize that having you in Black Mountain has not only put you in danger's way, but you'll find out my dirtiest secret.

Three years ago, I killed a man. I didn't pull the trigger, but I may as well have. His name was Ezra Donati, and I ensured he was dead before I walked away. I didn't think anything would come of it because I had the power of my job to keep me safe. That is until the men of his organization found out who put the hit out on him.

And now, I'm on the run.

My body turns to ice as my mouth falls open in shock. Elian's dad. *Does that mean he knows who I am?* I know he mentioned his dad was killed, but he never explained anything more than that, and each time I do ask him anything, he changes the topic. My chest tightens with fear and confusion. If he knows who I am, he could hurt me. But then again, it's been almost a month since we've been intimate, and he hasn't done anything to make me feel as if I'm in danger.

Nothing makes sense.

My phone buzzes on the nightstand, and from my viewpoint, I can see his name flashing on my screen. My hand hovers over the device, and I consider my options. But in the end, I leave it to ring and pick up my father's letter once more.

I needed to stay hidden for some time to put everything in place to ensure you're not going to be pulled into the middle of this. That's done now. Midge will give you everything when the time is right.

It's time for me to do the right thing. Once they find me, they will kill me. I will give myself up because I'm guilty, but I needed you to know who I am before I take my final breath.

I'm no hero.

I'm not at all a good father, but I want you to know I love you. I've always loved you.

Whatever comes now is something I deserve. But I want you safe. Promise me you'll stay safe no matter what. Don't trust easily, because when you allow your heart to fall, your life will only follow along.

Please, Princess, be careful.

All my love,

Dad

My phone vibrates again, this time with a message, but everything is blurry as the tears I'd been holding back for so long rush down my cheeks. I'm about to pick up the device from my nightstand when my bedroom door flings open, and on the threshold is the man who's toyed with my body, played with my heart, and could most probably kill me because of my father.

"I've been trying to contact you," Elian tells me, his voice rigid, filled with something akin to fear, which makes no sense. *Why would he be afraid?* "We need to talk."

"You knew," I tell him as I push off the bed to stand. "You knew the letter I got is from my father." Anxious energy skitters through me as he inches forward. We're alone in the house; I know Aunt Midge isn't home. "How did you get in here?"

"Are you sure you want an answer to that?" he questions with an arched brow.

Probably not is my silent answer, but then I voice my response, "You knew who I was all this time." I fist my hands to stop them from shaking and hide them from his gaze, but Elian notices the movement.

"I did." He takes another step deeper into the bedroom, and I instinctively move back, slamming into the nightstand, which shatters the silence. Even though I'm sure he won't do anything to me, I still feel anxiety coil in my stomach.

"You haven't hurt me."

He shakes his head, dropping his stare to the carpet for a long while as if he's considering his response. But then he lifts his eyes to meet mine. "I can't."

"Why?" It's probably a stupid question to ask, but I can't stop myself from voicing it. I need to know what his intentions are because if he is here to kill me, I'd rather he get it over with.

"I wanted revenge for so long," Elian admits before settling on the small stool at my vanity. "I spent years waiting for the right moment, and when your mother came to me, I made a deal and got you, I thought I could make you hurt as much as your father hurt me."

"Deal? What deal, Elian?" This time, I'm the one moving toward him. I'm not sure how to feel at his admission. One part of me wants to know, and the other part, that stupid bitch wants to hide all the shit and fall into his arms.

Elian shrugs. "Pandora came to me three months ago, asking for my help to kill your father. Her anger and hatred at his cheating had her contacting me. She found me through your father's contacts. When she came to me, she asked me to put a bullet between his eyes, but in the interim, Senator Adam Davenport disappeared. My revenge ran deep, Arabella. Your dad killed mine."

"How could you even know that?"

"Your dad and mine were working together for a long while. But then your father decided to pull out of a deal with my dad. The thing is, my father's organization doesn't allow people to just walk away and live to tell the tale. I just didn't think Adam would fake his own death, send you over the edge, and that's how you'd get here."

I know Dad wasn't the best man in the world and he did things behind closed doors, but his admission has now been confirmed. Dad sat me down not long before his *death* and told me he wanted me to attend Black Mountain Academy. And that's what sparked a number of events that led me here.

"Why didn't you tell me?"

"What?" Elian chuckles. "That I wanted revenge for your father killing mine? Or perhaps that the moment I fucked you in my bedroom that first night, every thought of revenge went out the fucking window?"

My mouth falls open at his admission. I'm not sure what I was expecting, but that was most definitely not it. Yes, I wanted Elian to tell me why, to explain what's going on, but I didn't expect him to talk about us like that.

"This was a game to you." My voice cracks as the realization hits me right in the gut. All this time, I was falling for a liar. He's just as bad as my father. The men in my life have acted like heroes. It turns out they're anything but.

"It was." Elian nods, pushing to his feet, he stalks to the window close to me. His hands snake into the pockets of his slacks, and it's only then I realize he looks like he's dressed for a party. A crisp white button-up, along with the small, black bowtie, and a pair of shiny, black shoes complete his outfit. "I wanted to break you."

For a long time, I consider his admission. His words, the truth finally spilling free, hits me in the chest. An arrow right to my heart. I swallow past the lump in my throat, and I finally find the words. "You did."

His head drops, and from this angle, he looks like a broken man. He doesn't look like the strong, foreboding teacher who rules his classroom with authority. He also doesn't look like the man who made my body sing under his touch and tremble beneath his control.

"I want to mend you," he admits after a long silence. "I want to put you back together, mold you for me. I've craved you since the first taste, since the moment I laid eyes on you." He turns his head toward me, blue locking on gray. "I've ached for you every night we haven't been together. You were made for me, Arabella."

I shake my head slowly. "This can never work." I can't be with a man who did what he did. He lied to me, hid his demons from me when he drew mine out into the light. He knew everything about me while he kept his sordid secrets. "What else is there? Are you still hiding something?"

"I met with your mother last night, well ... I met with the man who'd been watching you." I drop into the chair at the window where I'm standing because my knees can no longer hold me. "I hired him to scare you, and I thought perhaps he would push you closer to calling your father. I didn't know you thought your father was really dead."

"My rapist. You had the man who violated me when I was younger stalk me?" My voice cracks, the pain of his admission breaking through my strength, and I can't pull in breaths.

"I didn't know he'd done that. Of course, he didn't admit it until last night when I killed him. It turns out your mother had told him to kick things up a notch. Which led to your underwear drawer being violated." Elian moves closer to me, his cologne engulfing me as he crouches down in front of me. His hands on either arm of the chair, but he doesn't touch me. He's close enough, but he doesn't make contact, which I'm thankful for. "I never meant to hurt you in that way." The raw honesty in his voice, in his eyes, steals my words.

The moment I blink, tears trickle down my cheeks. "You ... I was just a deal to you. Nothing ... Everything we've done. All this bullshit was all lies!" I shove at him, causing him to stumble backward. But Elian straightens, standing to his full height as I push off the chair and my small fists slam into his chest. "Fuck you! Fuck you!"

Tears stream down my cheeks as my heart breaks, and my throat closes from screaming so loudly. My vision is dimming around me, and all I see are those fucking blue eyes.

"We're done! Do you hear me? We are done!"

"My little deviant," he says, the corner of his mouth tilting into a sardonic smirk as he allows me to punch him in the chest. "You think you can walk away from me…" Elian shakes his head. "There's no escaping what we are."

"It's as easy as saying it's over now," I insist, but even as I utter the words, I don't believe them. I push away from him, standing at the window, leaning against the cool glass, but nothing can calm my erratic, shattering heart.

Elian stares at me. With seemingly controlled steps, he eats up the distance between us and stops a hair's breadth away from me. He's so close I can feel his heat. I can smell the masculine scent I've come to love, and he leans in so his mouth is feathering along mine.

"Nothing between us can ever be over. You

might *think* it is, but I don't lose."

"This time, you did," I bite out, trying to fight off the need to fall into his arms. The thought of my father sending out an order to have Elian's dad murdered breaks my heart. But Elian could've told me the truth.

"I'm not giving up, Arabella. Ever." He presses his lips against mine for just a second before he pulls away and stalks off, leaving me shivering from the cold of his absence.

AHREN

He's going to be fucking angry when he walks in here. I settle into the wingback chair and wait. My ankle resting on the opposite knee, I sip the bourbon from one of his finest tumblers and think about everything he told me.

Killing Arabella's mother won't go down well, but I have a feeling she's going to hate him because he didn't tell her the truth. She wasn't close to her mother, that was apparent. But the fact that my brother didn't consult me on his little plan doesn't sit well with me.

I should wait to give him shit about it, but I can't. I've kept my own secrets he won't like, so I can't blame him. The buzzer sounds, which has me on my feet. Confusion settles when

I make my way to the door to find *her* at the entrance. The girl I had bouncing on my dick for months before Elian and I took her to my room one night. I'd filmed her while my brother watched from the corner like a voyeur.

"What are you doing here?"

Big hazel eyes lock on mine. Regan's grin turns sinister when she pushes by me, stalking into Elian's house. When he arrives, he's going to lose his shit. I follow her into the living room where she perches her ass on the sofa.

"You have to leave," I bite out.

"I'm not going anywhere until he gives me the video." She looks like she's about to set out demands when she pulls a phone from her pocket and slides it across the table toward me. "I have something to barter with."

Picking it up, I take in the photo, still unsure where she's going with this. I recognize the man immediately, but I'm not sure why she's got a photo of Adam Davenport on her phone.

"Elian's not going to give a shit about your lies." I toss the phone at Regan, and it bounces on the cushions beside her.

She sits back, her smile only broader as she

regards me. "You were always more fun than your brother," she informs me. "What happened to you, Ahren?"

Folding my arms across my chest, I narrow my eyes, wondering what she's playing at, but I respond anyway. "I grew up. Now leave."

"Like I said, I'm not going anywhere without that video."

"What's going on?" Elian's voice comes from behind me, and I find him standing at the threshold of the room. The moment I step aside, his gaze turns to rage. "What the fuck are you doing in my house?"

"I want the video."

"That video is to ensure you didn't come back. Seems like I need to post it all over the fucking internet since you broke the agreement." His words are cold, drenched in anger as he stops beside me.

"I've brought something for you though. In exchange for the video, I can give you something you've wanted for a long while," Regan says, pushing to her feet as she stalks toward Elian.

"What could you have that I would possibly want?" He sounds as doubtful as I felt, but after seeing the photo, I have a feeling Regan knew what she was doing. I also have an inclination that she's about to throw Elian off his usual control streak.

"You know, I've watched you with women," she says as she watches him with amusement. "In the darkness, I hid away, watching how you fucked them, and even though I had Ahren," she tells him, her gaze flicking to mine before she looks back at Elian. "You were always my goal."

"That's not going to happen. Ever. So, get your fairytale dreams out of that psychotic head of yours."

"Oh, that's okay, because I've seen you with *her*. Even with Tommy following her around, she still ran to you."

This time, Elian's rage shudders through the room. It's as if it is its own entity because he's in front of her in seconds, his hand wrapped around her neck, practically lifting her onto her tiptoes, but Regan laughs.

"What the fuck did you just say?"

"Oh, I met Tommy when I went to Miami to find out what it is you needed this girl for,"

Regan tells him, and I have a feeling if she continues, he will end her life. "He and I had fun toying with your little schoolgirl."

"You're a sick bitch," Elian growls, the feral sound reverberating through his throat. I'm beside him within two steps, my hand on his arm, which he attempts to shake off, but I'm not allowing my brother to do this.

"Listen to me, if you do this, you're only going to lose Arabella for good."

"There's no fucking point. She hates me," he grits out, sending shock flowing through me. "She told me she doesn't want me."

"And your anger needs to calm the fuck down, brother," I tell him. "Look at me." My voice is calm, but internally, I'm panicking. Elian's temper hasn't always been his strong suit, and losing Arabella could send him over the edge. "Regan has information on Adam Davenport," I tell him, hoping it will calm him the fuck down.

And it works.

He releases the girl and glares down at her. "I want everything, and you'll get your fucking video." I always knew Regan was in love with my brother. She was convinced he'd see her as a woman one day, but I know Elian, and he would never have gone for her. She's not his type, besides the fact that she's crazy.

My brother glances at me, offering me a nod to make the call we promised we'd do if she ever returned. I leave them to talk and head into the kitchen to call the hospital. Regan needs therapy. I'm not sure what kind, but I explain that she's a danger, and they confirm they're on their way.

When I get back to the living room, I witness the exchange. Regan's given Elian the details for Adam Davenport, while she's holding onto a flash drive I'm almost certain is empty. But she doesn't know it, and she's not asked to check it. Maybe she knows there's no video on there. Perhaps she's only here to see Elian.

A few moments of silence is as heavy as an anvil dropping on a wooden table. When the buzzer goes once more, I know who it is. As the men walk into the living room to get Regan, we're witness to expletives and cursing coming from her mouth that make me think of the goddamned *Exorcist* movie.

"You really know how to pick them," I tell Elian as he shuts the door, leaving us alone. He doesn't smile, but I don't expect him to. Losing Arabella must've hurt him a lot more than I have ever seen him.

"When we were back in Miami and Lacey cheated, I moved on. I was convinced I'd never love again," he tells me as he pours us both a drink. We settle in, and when Elian sets the bottle of bourbon on the table, I realize we're in for a late night.

"You love Arabella?"

He looks up at my question, his gaze locked on mine before he nods. "I didn't think it was possible. Now that I have Adam's location, I wonder if I should go to her with the details and see if she wants to talk to him."

"What did she say to you when you went to explain everything?" I ask before swallowing back a mouthful of amber liquid.

"Basically, she was angrier that I didn't tell her about my deal with her mother. It seems as if she knew about her dad's illegal dealings." He sits back, resting his head on the back of the couch, and I watch as he closes his eyes.

"Do you love her?" I ask again because I want to hear his words. I know my brother, and he's probably just avoiding the question because he does in fact love her, but he needs to admit it. If he can't, then it's pointless.

Silence hangs in the air amongst us. The tension radiating from him is stifling. I want so much to see him happy. He deserves it, but with his stubborn personality and Arabella being hurt by his actions, it seems almost impossible.

"I want so badly to bend her over my desk and fuck her senseless," he tells me, but he doesn't look up. I can't help but grin at him. One thing I've learned over the years about Elian Donati is that he uses sex as his way to communicate. "I made love to her, at the cabin."

"What?" This has me sitting up in my seat, shock rattling through me.

This time, he does look at me, a small smirk playing on his mouth. "Yeah," he says before swallowing his drink and reaching for the bottle to pour another one. "I fucking love her. As stupid as it sounds, I do."

"It's not stupid."

"It is. It's too soon, and now there may

not even be a chance." He shakes his head as he pours before setting the open bottle down, nudging it toward me in offering. "I love her."

"Then fight for her."

"She needs space," he informs me before knocking back another drink, and I grab the bottle, knowing I'm going to have to keep up with him tonight because that's what we do. We may not be blood, but he's my brother, and I will not let him drown his sorrows on his own.

"Then fight tomorrow, or the next day. Don't let this slip you by."

"Are you wanting me married off to a girl who's barely nineteen so you can go running around with bikers?" His question stills me, but when I glance at him, I find him grinning. "Asshole. I know you're going to go, and I wish you luck. Just don't be a stranger," he tells me, lifting his glass in a *cheers* toward me.

"You know I can never leave your ass completely." I chuckle. "What would you do without me?" Shrugging, I knock back my drink before pushing to my feet. Time for the hard stuff. I grab the Patron and set it between us with shot glasses. "How about a goodbye drinking night with your brother?"

With a laugh, Elian nods, sitting on the edge of the sofa, and he joins me in the first of many shots tonight. I'll have to say goodbye to Arabella soon as well. And that's not something I'm looking forward to. Because if my brother's asshole ways are anything to go by, she'll probably kick his ass to the curb someday.

I can just hope I'm wrong.

ELIAN

When I reach the meeting spot in the middle of nowhere, I pull out the gun I brought with me. The one I planned on killing Adam with. When I walked out of Black Mountain and came out here to see if the man who killed my father would show up, I didn't know what I would do.

Killing him would mean I would forever have the guilt of hurting Arabella's father. But shooting Adam Davenport would also ensure I got my revenge. But as I stand here waiting for him, I realize I need to make a choice.

What means more to me at this point—the woman who stole my heart, or the man who stole my father. Killing her mother hasn't left me with any guilt. Pandora hated everyone she came into contact with, including her daughter. And when I pulled the trigger, I most certainly didn't expect to see Arabella's tears, and I didn't.

The thought of her being alone at school irks me. Even though Ahren is meant to watch over her, at a distance, all I can do is hope she doesn't run. I wanted to tell her I'd be back, but I couldn't. I needed to do this before I went back there. Before I made my appearance back in her life.

"You came."

I turn to face Adam Davenport. The man looks aged, like he's been having countless sleepless nights. Perhaps he has. Guilt has eaten away at him, and now that we're meeting face to face, I wonder if he sees my father in me.

"I did."

"You brought a gun," he observes, his gaze flicking between my face and the weapon in my hand. "I wanted to tell you how sorry I am. There was a lot that you didn't know about him."

"I didn't come here to talk about my father. I came here to keep a promise." I step toward him and notice the glint of fear that flicks in his eyes as he regards me. "Your daughter is mine. I'm not giving up on her, no matter how many times she may send me away."

He looks at me then, and I lift the gun, pointing it at him. My finger lingers over the trigger, and for a moment, I wonder if he'll run. But he doesn't.

His question stills me. "Do you love her?"

Do I?

Yes.

"I do," I affirm. "I love her more than I've loved any woman before, and I know I'll love her until my final breath." There's no lie in my voice, in my words. Arabella is mine and she will always be mine.

"I want her safe." His voice cracks, and I see the shimmering emotion sparkling in his eyes. "I want her taken care of for the rest of her days." Even though this man had my father killed, his love for his daughter is endless. Even looking down the barrel of a gun, facing death, all he's concerned about is her safety, her happiness.

"I can do that." I lower my hand. "On one condition."

His eyes widen as he regards me.

"Anything."

"You pay for your sins," I tell him with conviction in my tone. I came her for revenge. I drove all this way, faced the man before me, and I am not someone who walks away empty handed.

Adam looks at me, and I can tell there is turmoil dancing in his mind. He doesn't know what to do, how to repent. But I know. I'm well versed in seeking salvation. Only, I found mine with a beautiful woman waiting in Black Mountain for me.

"Anything. Just make sure Arabella is alive, safe, and happy. I want her to be loved. Give her everything she deserves. And tell her I love her." He trembles, but I'm not sure if it's fear, or something else that takes a hold of him.

I nod, and then I get my revenge.

ARABELLA

School.

Classes.

But no Elian Donati.

It's been a week since my world imploded, yet he's nowhere to be seen. I've had my ear pods in every day, ignoring everyone and anyone who would want to talk to me. The playlist has been depressing, heart-wrenching songs have been on repeat. With Tommy gone and my mother murdered by the man I'd been sleeping with, the only part of my past still somewhere in the world is my father.

Forgiveness is a heavenly virtue I don't possess. The men in my life have lied to me, hurt me, and kept me in the dark while promising to care for me. Elian may not have said those three words I longed to hear, but he did act as if I were his. And for a long while, I believed it. I *felt* it right down to my bones.

Right now, I'm no longer sure about anything. I haven't seen him at school, so I'm not sure where he's gone, but if he's decided just to leave Black Mountain without even saying goodbye, I need to move on.

At least, that's what I tell myself.

Elian's not a man you *just get over*. He's everything, all-consuming, and I allowed him to take every part of me with him. And all he left behind were memories that slowly etch deeper grooves into my heart as each day passes.

When I make my way downstairs, I find Aunt Midge sitting at the kitchen table. She looks tired, and I wonder why she doesn't retire. It's not like she needs to work. She glances up and smiles.

"Just the girl I wanted to talk to."

Sliding into a chair, I attempt a smile, which I'm almost sure comes out as a grimace. "Me? What did I do this time?"

She shakes her head, sliding a folder toward

me. "This is yours, and I wanted to give it to you as a graduation present. I know you came to Black Mountain because of lies and betrayal, and you haven't had many chances to just enjoy your time here. But with prom coming up and then your graduation, I thought it would be good for you to have something to look forward to."

I open it, finding a set of keys along with a card, which has the date and time to be home to meet one of the newest up-and-coming designers from New York. I look up, finding Aunt Midge smiling at me.

"What is this?"

"I've spoken to my contacts, and I've heard all the buzz is around Shisha who is one of the most sought-after designers, and she'll be designing your prom dress." Her grin is sparkling as she stares at me, and I feel bad because I really didn't want to party with everyone when my heart feels like it's been ripped out and stomped on.

"I … I wasn't going to go," I finally tell her, tears brimming my lashes, turning my vision blurry with emotion.

Aunt Midge takes my hand in hers. "You know, your father was a difficult man. Your mother was as well. We never got on, but there's one thing I learned from them. Even in their biggest fights, they still did what was expected of them."

"And that's why I hated my life," I counter, "Posing for cameras, smiling when my heart was aching," I tell her. "It's not who I am."

She nods slowly. "I know how that feels. That's why I moved out here," she informs me. "But I would like you to go to the prom, just because it's a special day. Do it for me?" I don't know what to say to her. "I can't promise that your life will be perfect from here on out, but perhaps I can get your dad to just give you a call."

"You knew he was alive?"

"Not at first, but he contacted me a month ago to tell me everything. I'm angry, I want to kill him myself, but I think it would be good for you."

Shrugging, I try once more to smile, but fail. "I guess. I just hate all men."

Her gaze holds me hostage, keeping me

from turning away before she asks the question I've been trying to find an answer to. "Do you hate him?"

"Of course, I hate dad for—"

"Not him," Midge interrupts, causing an image of Elian to spark into my thoughts like a photograph my mind took when I last saw him. "Do you truly hate Elian?"

I open my mouth to say *yes,* but then I can't voice it. Because I know I don't hate him. Not truly. I love him, and that's what hurts me so much. He could've spoken to me, given me the truth instead of hiding everything from me.

"How do you know about Elian and me?" Shock laces my words as I stare at my aunt.

She grins as if she knows everything that happens in this town. And she probably does. "When I saw you with Ahren, I thought you may be dating him, but then when you didn't bring him home and I still saw you around him, I figured there was more to the story."

"You're far too wise, Aunty Midge," I tell her, a soft smile curling my lips.

"I try," she informs me with a laugh, but then her expression turns serious. "You know, your parents weren't good people," Midge says, and I nod because I was never convinced I came from innocents. I'm a deviant, which makes them just as bad. Probably worse because they've had more time to cultivate the sinister things they've done.

"I know."

"Your father was involved in illegal dealings for most of his life, and your mother, my sister, she was … God, she deserves anything that's coming to her. Since we were kids, she had stolen, lied, and she'd hurt everyone in her path to get where she is. I'm not telling you this to hurt you."

"I would rather know the truth than to believe lies." This time, I know it's the truth. Knowing where I've come from will ensure I don't turn out like them. And that's what I needed from Elian, the truth.

"Don't push him away," my aunt tells me. "I've regretted divorcing your uncle for so long, and look at me, this lonely old lady, holding onto a house that's filled with memories I lost a long time ago." She laughs, but it's the first time I truly look into her eyes and see the pain, the heartbreak.

"I'll think about it. And anyway, you're not lonely. I'm here." I push to my feet and round the table to give her a hug. I'm not sure how to get through heartbreak, but for now, I'll keep my aunt close and hopefully learn how to forgive Elian for lying and for leaving me. Even though I sent him away.

On the way to school, I get lost in the lyrics of "So Far Away" by Martin Garrix, Jamie Scott, and David Guetta on repeat. It's the only song that has kept my tears at bay but still causes my chest to tighten, reminding me that *he* did exist.

ELIAN

Exile.

I feel like I'm in fucking exile.

When I spoke to Ahren, I wanted to ensure he knew I wasn't going after Adam to kill him. As much as I wanted my revenge, my brother made me see that taking Adam's daughter for my own would be the best revenge. She'll be happy beside me, and if he ever came near us, I would most certainly end him.

But that's not what's bothering me. The thought of her being alone, without me, has me on edge. I should apologize, I should also explain myself, but I'm not good with letting my feelings show. The most I've ever bared myself to someone was when I was practically engaged. And look how that turned out. But then again, I know Arabella isn't my past, she's my future. She just has to see it that way.

The plan I have set in place is going to be easy to pull off, but if it actually works is going to be the miracle. Which brings me to the house I've been at so many times, but I've never once come inside and spoken to Midge.

She opens the door for me, and she doesn't look angry, which has my breath whooshing from my lungs in one fell swoop. There's a small smile on her face, and I wonder if she's enjoying me coming to her with my tail between my legs.

"Mr. Donati," Midge greets me, her hand offered, and I accept. We shake on it, and I feel like this is a woman I can get used to. She's older, possibly in her late forties, but she comes across as someone who's still got her youth waiting to be explored.

"Thank you for seeing me," I tell her as she ushers me inside. "I don't want to stay long in the event that Arabella gets home early."

"Don't you worry about my niece." She waves her hand in the air as if this is just a normal occurrence in her world. She leads me into the living room I'm almost sure has been styled by a team of designers. The cream colors with pops of purple and blue in the cushion fabrics, along with the throw rug, show off a professional eye to the room. "So, have a seat and tell me what's going on."

I settle in, and I'm not sure I want to tell this woman I shot her sister. I didn't check if Pandora actually died, but I did walk out, leaving her bleeding. The cleanup crew confirmed two bodies, but knowing Pandora, she probably had someone take her place. That is, if she survived my shot.

I breathe deeply before I start. "I wanted to know if I even have a chance at forgiveness from Arabella if I spoke to her. If I were to explain why I did what I did, perhaps she'd see it my way."

"My niece is stubborn, and I have a feeling you're the same," Midge muses, her smile brightening her face. "But I think if you dropped to your knees to apologize for your lies, she'll come around."

"I made a mistake. I dealt with her as if she were a pawn in a game, and at first, she was."

Even as the words leave my mouth, I can hear just how bad that sounds. "I've done some terrible things in my life, but this was by far the worst."

"Even after killing my sister?" she challenges, giving me pause. "You're a good shot, Mr. Donati," Midge informs me. "I've always had a tail on her. My business calls for being careful of people, especially family."

"I—"

"Please, don't apologize. That woman got everything that's been coming to her. Sending her daughter away, bartering her life was nothing compared to what I've witnessed. Too bad you didn't get Adam while you were at it," she tells me with a grin on her face that shocks me silent.

All this time, I thought she was just an older woman running a business. I didn't realize she was so in tune with what's been going on in her family. Living in Black Mountain isolates you from the rest of the world.

"I'm making Arabella go to the prom," Midge tells me. "I would recommend you make an appearance, and you can show her what you feel. Telling that girl will not change her mind. She's too fucking stubborn. But if you show her, then she may just give you a chance."

Her advice slowly sinks in, but even as she tells me what to do, I'm still of two minds about this. Going to a senior prom isn't exactly what I had in mind when I chose to do this, but if I'm going to get *my* girl, then I'm going to have to sacrifice my pride and do anything to get her back. Because I will do anything for her.

"You know, Elian," Midge says. "When I first noticed her smiling all the time, and her excited exploits, I was worried she'd end up in the same situation she was in back home. But she's not the same. She's changed, grown up. It was only when she spent the past few days indoors and her friend Marleigh came to me and told me about you and her, that's when I realized the truth."

"What truth is that?"

"My niece is in love with you," Midge informs me nonchalantly as if it's normal for her to say something like that. Her words cause me to still in shock. "And I have a feeling you're in love with her, or you wouldn't be here."

I nod slowly. "I am. I haven't told her yet. I haven't even gotten myself to believe it." And I still don't. Even when I told Ahren, it was merely to get him off my back, but now that I look at the older woman staring at me with a piercing gaze, I realize I'm going to have to give Arabella everything.

If she's going to forgive me, I'm going to have to admit how I feel about her. And that means I'm going to have to say those three words to her.

"Are you ready for this?" Midge's question lingers in my mind before she says, "Because you have to ask yourself, if you're not willing to open up to her, you won't get her back, and it would be best to walk away."

That causes me to snap my gaze to hers. "I can't walk away from Arabella." That's not a lie. I tried. She told me to leave, and I did, but I didn't go far.

"Then you know what you need to do."

I nod.

I do.

I'm going to get my little deviant back.

ARABELLA

I feel out of place.

But I know I belong.

For the first time in my life, I truly belong. The problem is, he's not here. When I walked into history class and didn't see Elian at his desk, my stomach dropping to my feet. Not that I expected him to return to Black Mountain after everything that happened, but deep down, I thought he would at least say goodbye. Even if he was angry, all I wanted was an explanation.

Why save me when all he ever wanted was to hurt me?

"Christ almighty." Marleigh's overexcited voice startles me. I turn to face her, giving her the first glimpse of the dress. The soft material hugs me like a second skin. Deep red, the color of wine, clings to my hips and glides down my arms. The delicate material hangs off the shoulder, giving way as the dip plunges down toward my lower back where the zipper comes together over the curve of my butt.

Black lace inches its way over the edges of the hem and neckline as the floor length offers a slit that slides all the way to my upper thigh, gifting anyone a view of my tanned leg as I take a step. I know Elian would have a coronary if he were here. He never liked others looking at me, besides Ahren of course.

"Hey," Marleigh says, dragging my attention back to her. "He's the asshole for leaving you." She knows about my relationship with Elian. When he left, I told her everything, but what I didn't admit was that I had fallen in love with him. I wanted a final kiss but he never offered it. Instead, he stole my heart and soul, and he never returned them when he spun on his heel and left me staring at his back.

"I know." Even as I voice the words, I don't believe them. Neither does my friend. We've come a long way since my first day at Black

Mountain Academy. And I'm thankful she's been by my side.

"Come on," she says, leading me out into the hallway and down the steps until we get to the door where she has a sleek, silver Audi R8 waiting.

"Shit," I curse, taking in the beautiful vehicle. "This is pure sex."

"Then you've been having the wrong sex, gorge," Marleigh says with a laugh. I roll my eyes at her response. She's draped in floor-length, silver satin that hugs her every curve. The halter neck holds the dress up, while the cut-out diamond shape at her chest offers a glimpse of cleavage.

"Oh please, I just didn't go sleeping with a college boy every day after school," I tease, causing her to blush. She shrugs me off, and we make our way to the car where I slip into the passenger seat.

"Yeah, and I haven't been shacking up with a hot teacher," Marleigh retorts playfully, which only feels like a kick in the gut. "Shit, I'm sorry."

"It's okay. I have to get over it. Right?"

She shakes her head sadly before pressing

the start button. The stereo's on, playing "Bad Guy" by Billie Eilish. It throbs through the speakers, and I smile. "See? Music is the remedy." She winks before pulling out onto the road and taking us toward the school.

I haven't told her how difficult it's been without him. I haven't confessed just how painful it is to be at school, walking around campus without Elian near. I'm not sure where he's gone, and I haven't seen Ahren in weeks, which feels far too long, and I miss him and his friendship.

By the time we reach the academy, I'm less nervous, but I'm having second thoughts about being here, yet Marleigh doesn't allow me to race home. Not like I could in these fucking heels. So, I follow her up to the entrance which has been set up like a fairytale ball.

"Smile, pretty girls." The familiar rumble of Ahren has me spinning on my heels to find him standing behind me. He's dressed in black leather, as usual, but it's the look in his eye that makes my heart settle in my chest. He makes me feel like being home. Like a brother would calm my crazy, that's what Ahren does for me.

"You're here." It comes out as a disbelieving whisper, but he hears me. Ahren loops his arm through mine, and we head inside, but he doesn't explain why he's here. I want to ask, it burns the tip of my tongue, but I don't want to sound like a crazy ex-girlfriend. They've already had one of those, and I don't plan on being another.

Ahren doesn't stop until we get to the bar which, thankfully, is serving drinks. Even though everything is non-alcoholic, I grab one and swallow down two mouthfuls. I can't describe what it feels like seeing Elian's brother here and knowing he's not close by.

"What are you doing here?" I ask Ahren as he leads me onto the dance floor, ignoring Marleigh who's staring at us with her mouth agape in shock at the turn of events. The song changes before he can respond, and I'm taken into his arms, and we slowly move across the floor. Even though there are a few couples already dancing, it's as if we're the only people here.

"He's ..." Ahren shakes his head. "Don't Give Me Those Eyes" by James Blunt screams at us, and I wonder if it's *him* speaking to me from a goddamned song. I've lost my fucking mind. "He didn't want to leave."

"Well, he did," I bite out, anger taking over the sadness that's been holding me hostage since Elian left me standing in the darkness. "He doesn't deserve my tears." Even as I grit the words through clenched teeth, I feel the burn of salty emotion about to take over.

"He doesn't. But that doesn't mean he doesn't want them." The music slows, and as it comes to an end, Ahren doesn't release me. His arms are warm, affectionate, and for a moment, I think he's going to kiss me. But he doesn't lean in, he doesn't capture my mouth like Elian used to do. He merely stares at me. "My brother did tend to enjoy making girls cry."

I watch the younger Donati, and I can't help but sneer at his response. "He's an asshole."

"Why?" he challenges as he spins me across the dance floor when another song starts up, and we weave in between the other couples, and I'm lost in the way we're moving effortlessly. "Because he saved you? Or because he chose to leave the life that he built behind to ensure you're able to graduate?"

I look around, taking in all the happy faces, and I wish I could be one of them. But I also ponder Ahren's questions for a long moment. I don't know how to answer him without breaking down. It hasn't been long, but it feels as if a part of me has been torn from my chest. I lock my gaze on Ahren's before I finally whisper the words I've hidden deep in my heart since his kiss, "Because he left me."

"I could never leave you, even if I wanted to," the familiar rumbled, yet husky growl comes from behind me, causing me to spin on my heel, leaving Ahren's arms to find those iridescent blue eyes I've come to love.

"You're here." The words are whispered on a gasp, a breath of shock at him standing here, looking like a hero, a white knight. Dressed in a black tux that looks like it's been tailored perfectly to his frame, a deep-red button-up, which eerily matches my dress, and a tie that shimmers, making it seem as if the night sky has been folded and bound into a knot just for him.

The corner of his mouth tilts upward, and I'm lost in the endless ocean pools that have captured me since the first time I saw them. He doesn't speak, but his gaze holds me steady as if I'm a possession, and I suppose I am. Elian Donati owns me, and I'm okay with that.

"Thank you," he says, looking over my shoulder at Ahren who bows out like a gentleman taking his leave. Then those blues are on my grays. "I should never have left you like that."

"No, you shouldn't have."

"I had spilled blood. I lost control, and being around you would've just made it worse. I felt guilty for what I did." It's the first time that I see Elian unsure of himself. Granted, he's talking about killing a man, but he did it to protect me.

"You thought I would judge you for saving my life?"

Fury blazes in his stare, and I wonder if he's recalling the shitshow that went down. The asshole was stalking me, doing things with my underwear, putting fear into my mind. And Elian ended it, even though he started it.

"I'll never apologize."

"I didn't ask you to," I reply. "I needed you." My admission causes my cheeks to heat, the blush burning along my skin down to my chest.

"I don't like this dress," Elian grunts, as he sways me along the dance floor to the song. "Too many men can see what's mine."

"Am I though?" I challenge him, locking my gaze on his. "Am I yours?"

"If you ever doubted it," he tells me. "I'm here to show you that you have nothing to doubt." His mouth crashes on mine, and I feel as if the whole senior year has stopped all movement and I'm the center of attention. Usually, I'd pull away and hide from the eyes on me, but right now, all I want is Elian to devour me whole.

There are stares from other students, whispers as we move through the crowd, but I don't care. I no longer fear what people say or think about me and the choice I've made. And it seems Elian doesn't either.

As the song fades into another, Elian laces his fingers with mine, and he leads me out into the sparkling night. Between the stars and the fairy lights that illuminate the path leading up to the entrance, we're bathed in a soft, yellow glow.

Elian turns to me, his eyes shimmering as he regards me. "I will never in my life lie to you or hide anything from you again. I've lost you once. I'm not prepared to do it again."

I bite the inside of my cheek to keep from grinning. "Are you trying to tell me I'm stuck with you, Mr. Donati?" The challenge in my words causes his eyes to glimmer with desire.

"Oh, that's exactly what I'm telling my beloved little deviant."

My mouth falls open, but I shut it quickly, almost as if I didn't just hear what he said, but Elian's more perceptive than that. With me, it's as if he can read my mind.

"I love you, Arabella," he confesses. "And I'm not prepared to ever watch you leave my life. Never again." My heart skips multiple beats from his confession, but I'm grinning from ear to ear.

"Then you better be on your best behavior, Mr. Donati," I tell him. "And don't ever leave me." This time, I snake my arms around his waist, tilting my head backward so I can look into those blue eyes. "I love you too, by the way," I admit, my cheeks burning from embarrassment and nervousness.

"Then it seems we're stuck with each other." And he kisses me against the cool brick wall where nobody else can see us. He consumes me with everything he has, and I know tonight, he'll once again make love to me.

And I welcome it—tonight, and for the rest of my nights well into the future.

EPILOGUE

ELIAN

Even though it's not entirely the last day of classes, I'm here to collect my belongings. I've enjoyed saying goodbye to my students. From tomorrow, they'll have a brand-new teacher to deal with. When I went to Dawson and asked him to allow me to resign, he did ask why, and I had to explain that I'd fallen for one of the students. I didn't go into detail, but I have a feeling he knew who it was.

The whispers had been going around since prom, and I needed a new start with Arabella. Since she's decided to go to England for university, I told her I'm not allowing her to go on her own. Which brings me back to the last afternoon I'll ever be in this class. The door clicks, and I grin. Glancing to the left, I see Arabella walk toward me in her school uniform.

"Hello, Mr. Donati," she greets in a seductive tone that has my cock jolting against my zipper. "I figured I needed some … detention," she says, running her nail from the knot in my tie down to where the pointed end stops at my belt buckle.

"Bend over this fucking desk, Ms. Davenport," I order, my voice already husky with need to be inside her. Like the good girl she is, Arabella obeys, leaning her slender frame over the edge of my desk. Her skirt hikes up, just far enough to gift me a view of the bottom curve of the cheeks of her ass. "Where are your panties, deviant?"

"Oops, I think I lost them, Mr. Donati," she coos in a voice that ignites my blood, causing it to turn to lava in my veins. I shift the hem of her skirt, shoving it over her hips to find her bare.

My hand comes down on her ass, harshly, echoing through the room until I bring it down again on the other cheek. Squeals of pleasure tumble from her lips, and I continue my assault of her pert little butt.

"Elian, please," she whimpers as I turn her ass cheeks bright red. My handprint is etched into her flesh, and I can't help but smile.

"When you scream, it will be with me inside you," I tell her before unzipping my slacks, fisting my cock, and lining it up with her entrance. I don't have to wait because she's drenched. My cock sinks into her in one long thrust, which has my eyes rolling back in my head. The pleasure that zips through every inch of me causes a growl to fall from my lips. I reach for her neck, holding her against me, feeling every part of her tremble at the nearness.

"Oh god, you're so deep," Arabella moans when I slide into her, taking her harshly, claiming my little deviant once more. With every thrust, I confirm wordlessly she is mine. She disappeared from my life for a short moment, but she will never leave my life again.

"You. Are. Mine." Every word is enunciated by the thrust of my hips before I bite down on her earlobe, tugging the soft flesh, causing her cunt to tighten around my shaft, and I drown in her sweetness. We're so close she's molded to me, and with every pulse, I feel the emotion taking hold of me. My chest bursts, the black heart I long since hid away fills with her light. I tried to fight it, but I fell for her.

"I've always been yours," she hisses as I tug her hair, my free hand gripping her throat and squeezing, which only makes the slick warmth of her body pulse around my shaft as if she's milking my fucking soul from my body.

"Happy Graduation, little deviant," I murmur as I fuck her harder, faster, until we're both shattering, splintering as she calls out my name for the whole fucking school to hear, and I grunt my release inside her.

ARABELLA

Two months later

Nothing in this world could've prepared me for the journey that Black Mountain brought me. It wasn't just eye-opening. I grew up, became a woman. I'm no longer fearful of the future—I'm looking forward to it. And as I say goodbye, I wonder what would've happened to me if I never came here.

The man beside me wouldn't be in my life, and he wouldn't be holding my hand. The shiny promise ring on my left ring finger wouldn't be glittering for the world to see. And I would never have thought I would be okay with a man who killed my mother. But when I thought about his admission, when he explained how she so easily bartered me as if I were a possession, I knew my instinct was right—she never loved me.

"Are you ready?" Elian asks from beside me.

Nodding, the excitement has now taken over, and I'm ready to leave. When I glance over my shoulder, I wave at Aunt Midge who's grinning from ear to ear. Apparently, she spoke some sense into Elian, and that's how he ended up coming to prom. I'm thankful for her. Even though we haven't heard from my dad again, I know if he were to ever come near us, he wouldn't live to tell the tale. Either that, or he'd be in prison.

Two wrongs don't make a right. Even though he knew where Dad was, he chose me instead of the revenge he'd been seeking since his father died. I've found someone special, and I'm lucky.

Elian's hand lands on my thigh, and he gives it a squeeze as we head out onto the highway which will take us to the airport. Behind us, Black Mountain shrinks the farther away we get from it, and I wonder momentarily if we'll ever see it again. Since Ahren has left to move to Arizona, and my aunt is thinking of moving to New York, there's not much for the small town to come back to.

"I love you, little deviant," Elian tells me, the confidence in his voice sending my stomach into whirls of excitement.

"And I love you, Mr. Donati," I murmur in return, earning my leg another squeeze. Time to make new memories and break so many more rules than we've already done.

THE END

ACKNOWLEDGMENTS

I cannot believe this book is done. It's been one heck of a rollercoaster! Thank you to the amazing Alta Hensley for telling me about this super fun project, and a HUGE thank you to Jenika Snow for inviting me to be a part of the Black Mountain Academy!

Thank you to four special ladies, to the awesome Candice Royer for helping me with ALL the freaking edits. This was most definitely a tough one. To Allyson and Nikki for their BETA reading skills, as well as Ally for falling in love with Mr. Donati. And also a MASSIVE thank you to Marjorie for stepping in to proofread at the last minute. I know I may have melted your Kindle, but Mr. Donati says *thanks!* ;)

To my ADULT, Caroline for putting up with my bullshit.

To my hubster who makes the dinner and ensures I have alcohol on hand while I'm on deadline. You may not be my teacher, but you're my everything. Love you madly!

The Street Team, you ladies work your ass off to get my name out there, thank you. From the bottom of my little black heart, THANK YOU!

My Deviants!! This group is like my own personal form of therapy. Thank you!! There is never a dull moment, and that's what makes me thankful for your love and support. It's not easy working with the intense stress and deadlines, but you always seem to brighten my day!

To my fellow authors who are there with advice, support, and just a general pick me up. Thank you. It means more to me than you know. Thank you for sharing my work with your readers, and giving me a friendship that is second to none.

To the bloggers, you ladies read, read, read, support, post, review, and you do it with a smile. Thank you!! We wouldn't be here if it weren't for you, so keep what you're doing, we appreciate you! #AllBlogsMatter!

Lastly, to the readers, thank YOU! It's because of you I'm able to put out book after book. Giving you what you ask for, and hopefully making you excited about the next book. Thank you for your reviews, keeping them SPOILER FREE ;) But most of all, thank you for buying our books. For your support, love, and encouragement.

Mad love, D x

STALK ME

My exclusive reader group gets news on all up and coming releases, sales, and a chance at early ARC copy giveaways! Join us, we don't bite... hard ;)

Dani's Deviants
www.facebook.com/groups/danisdeviants/

Or sign up for my newsletter and get an exclusive novella not available for purchase anywhere!

Sign Up Now!
https://bit.ly/DaniVIPs

ALSO BY DANI RENÉ

It's Never Easy (Lady Boss Press)

Only One Night (Lady Boss Press)

Deviant (Black Mountain Academy)

Traction (KB Worlds)

Taboo Novellas

Sunshine and the Stalker (collaboration with K Webster)

His Temptation

Austin's Christmas Shortcake

Crime and Punishment (Newsletter Exclusive)

Malignus (Inferno World Novella)

Tempting Grayson

Gilded Sovereign Series

Cruel War (Book #1)

Volatile Love (Book #2)

Sins of Seven Series

Kneel (Book #1)

Obey (Book #2)

Indulge (Book #3)

Ruthless (Book #4)

Bound (Book #5)

Envy (Book #6)